Those Crazy 7 Years

OrangeBooks Publication

1st Floor, Rajhans Arcade, Mall Road, Kohka, Bhilai, Chhattisgarh 490020

Website: **www.orangebooks.in**

First Edition, 2025

ISBN: 978-93-5621-573-3

Price: Rs. 250.00

Printed in India

Those Crazy 7 Years

Subhransu Sekhar Ojha

Orange Books Publication
www.orangebooks.in

An Exquisite Journey from Friendship to Marriage

Author - Subhransu Ojha
Bhadrak, Odisha

Content

1

When the Heart Decides

Time was passing like a **brake-less vehicle**, as if there were no speed breakers on the road of life.

I still remember that day clearly. It was **mid-July 2005**. There was a big family function scheduled in her village, and all her family members, including her, had to travel from Bhubaneswar to their native place for 3–4 days.

The moment I heard this; my brain lit up like a person being revived by an electric shock.

My thoughts were racing, flooded with wild excitement.

It was scorching hot outside that day. I was on a bus, returning from college. Lost in thought, I unknowingly stepped off the bus, unaware that I had even reached my stop. I went home, dropped my college bag in my room, and quickly laid on my bed, mentally drilling into the possibilities of the next three days.

My heart was filled with plans. I was certain she would be equally thrilled. I rushed to the ground floor, to the local **STD booth**, to call her. I wanted to share everything before she left for the village.

It was a rare and precious chance to spend some time with her and I didn't want to waste it.

The phone rang.

"Hello..." she said, her voice as sweet and soothing as always.

I froze for a moment in excitement, just absorbing her voice. She repeated,

"Hello? Are you there?"

"Oh yes! Sorry... I was just... looking outside the booth," I stammered.

"It’s me, Subhransu."

Yes, I lied knowingly.

"What are you doing?" I asked.

"Just got freshened up after college. Was prepping for the evening."

"Hey, I have something really important and exciting to tell you!"

"Really? Oh wow, tell me fast, I'm so anxious to hear it!"

The eagerness in her voice sent a wave of joy through me. Without pausing, I poured out my entire plan, all my dreams for those upcoming days without a single full stop.

But then…

She put a **big full stop** to it all.

She flatly denied it. **"No. It's not possible."**

She was right, of course. But I was too excited to think straight. All I wanted was a day with her. Nothing serious. Nothing inappropriate.

I simply wanted her **time**, her **presence**, her **affection**. A peaceful, sacred moment with the person I loved. That was all.

I even wished she could return a day earlier from her village on the pretext of some urgent college work. That way, I could spend just **one magical day** with her.

I knew the family function was important, and I also knew her entire family wouldn't return early. So my plan was simple and subtle, **she'd return alone**, and we'd meet, talk, laugh, dream… together.

From sunrise to sunset, my mind was lost in a world of imagination, each moment filled with hopes and plans.

Roaming freely. Sitting together without fear. Maybe even at her home. Talking endlessly.

But she was terrified of the plan.

She was scared of the **neighboring aunty** whose window was just 4 feet away from hers. If that aunty saw us together in their house, it could spell disaster.

Still, I was adamant.

If I had imagined something, it had to come true. Such was the **crazy intensity** of my love back then.

Eventually, I convinced her.

She promised she'd return a day earlier, alone, using a believable excuse. I wasn't entirely happy that I'd get just one day with her, but it was better than nothing.

They left for the village.

What she didn't know was that I had also **skipped an important family get-together**, something I was expected to attend. I lied at home, pretending I had a lot of college assignments.

It was like missing a royal coronation.

My family was upset. But I didn't care. I wanted just that **one day** with her.

Two days later, she returned. It was around 4 PM.

I was already waiting at the **bus stop**, and the moment I saw her, I was overwhelmed. During those days, even talking openly wasn't easy. Shyness, hesitation, and the fear of misunderstanding were always present.

But love is an unspoken language.

Your eyes, your smile, your silence, they say what your words can't.

She could sense my excitement, and her **cute smile** said it all.

We chatted as we walked to her house. She told me how she managed to come early using the story we had crafted. She was tired from the 4-hour journey, so I asked her to rest while I completed some work.

Before leaving, I reminded her,

"I'll come at night. Everyone's returning tomorrow, so this is our only chance to meet."

She smiled nervously and nodded. She was scared but still agreed.

That night, I couldn't sleep.

I had **no mobile phone**. We had planned I'd ring her from an STD booth around **11:30 PM** as a signal that I was entering the colony.

I had even taken a rented house at that time, staying with my younger brother and a friend.

I fed them, helped them settle, and pretended to sleep. As the clock ticked toward 11:00 PM, my excitement soared. My heart was racing. Every minute felt like a lifetime.

Finally, I got up silently. Carefully.

I took out my bicycle and began riding toward her colony, about **7–8 kilometers away**.

The night was pitch dark. Silent. Haunting.

Suddenly, a chill ran through me.

What am I doing? In this dead of night? Is this safe?

For a moment, I felt like turning back. But then… I reminded myself:

"My intentions are pure. I'm not doing anything wrong."

I pedaled forward.

Lightning flashed. Thunder cracked. Rain started falling lightly. It didn't stop me.

I reached near the colony. It was near the National Highway. I began searching for an open STD booth, but everything was closed. After 15 minutes of anxious wandering, I found a **liquor shop** still open.

Desperately, I requested to make a single call.

After many questions, the shopkeeper agreed. I dialed her number. No answer. Tried again. Nothing.

I called her **20 times**. Still nothing.

My heart sank.

I sat there… hopeless… hurt. I had travelled all this way. For this.

But I wasn't ready to give up.

I entered the colony quietly. The **security guard** was asleep. Thank God. Her father was the **colony superintendent** any report from the guard could have been catastrophic.

I reached her building, hid behind a small flowering tree, and looked at the door.

The lights were on. The **main gate was locked** from inside.

I knocked. Nothing. I waited. I knocked again. Still nothing.

I was shattered. Came back to the National Highway.

I tried another STD booth. Still no response.

I stood near the liquor shop, heartbroken, feeling like a man without a home. As if I had been **divorced from existence**.

I thought of giving up. I cried like a child.

Even the shopkeeper offered me a drink out of sympathy.

I refused and said I don't take it.

Then, mustering every ounce of courage, I made one final attempt and proceeded to the colony again.

Again, she didn't respond.

Her door remained locked. The light still on. She had likely fallen asleep.

I was defeated.

I cried all the way back on the **national highway**, in the **rain**, with my tiny bicycle and a heart full of pain.

As I rode back, soaked and shivering in the midnight rain, something strange happened.

Right after crossing the flyover near Khandagiri, I spotted a small boy, barefoot, wearing a torn shirt, standing under a streetlight, looking up at the sky.

I stopped.

He noticed me, came closer, and said something that froze me.

“Bhaiya... Don’t cry. Your love is not lost. You are just being tested.”

I was stunned. How did he know?

Before I could respond, he ran off into the darkness.

I turned to look for him again, but he had vanished.

"I don’t know who he was, maybe just a poor child. Or maybe… something else. An angel in disguise? A message from the universe? Or perhaps… it was my own soul speaking to me, emerging from the deepest core of my heart, born from a hallucination… a fragile echo of the mental trauma I had just endured."

I smiled softly through my tears. Maybe this wasn’t the end of the road.

I kept turning that image around in my head, the barefoot child, the way he vanished into the night.

Sometimes, late at night, I would imagine seeing him in crowds, as if a small signal in the world tried to remind me: “Keep walking.” I never found him again, but the thought that someone, somewhere, watched over that broken boy stayed with me.

I thought that night was the end of it. I was wrong.

Sometimes the small kindnesses we ignore some advice, a stranger’s word, are what keep a person alive. Respect those moments.

Memories flooded my mind.

How we first met. Our bond. Our laughs. Our silent promises. Unknowingly I started drilling our past….

The First Day at Engineering College

It was ***July 2002****, around* ***11 in the morning****. The sun was ruthless, scorching everything below as if it had sprinkled droplets of fire from the sky.*

My father and I stood waiting at ***Baramunda Bus Stand*** *in Bhubaneswar for my cousin brother’s friend Chintu. It was the* ***first day of my engineering journey****.*

My mind was racing with a thousand thoughts: “What will the first day be like? Will I be ragged? Will seniors bombard me with questions? Are the students from Bhubaneswar fashionable and affluent? I know nothing about style; how will I fit in?”

*Just then, putting a full stop to my overthinking, a **two-wheeler zoomed in and stopped** right in front of us. The rider smiled and said to my father,*

"Uncle, Namaskar. I'm Chintu. I'll take you both to the engineering college."

Apparently, my cousin had arranged for him.

So off we went, on his miniature-magnitude two-wheeler.

A few minutes later, we arrived.

*And I was **stunned**.*

*It was majestic. The **lush campus**, high-tech infrastructure, **sprinklers dancing over green lawns**, flowering trees lining the walkways, it didn't look like a college. It looked like a **resort**.*

"This is an engineering college?" I thought to myself. "Wow... My father will be so proud. He'll go home and tell everyone, 'My son is studying in one of the best colleges!'"

*Amidst that joy, there was also anxiety about the ragging stories I'd heard. Still, the **admission process** went smoothly, and we returned home the same day.*

*Fifteen days later, I moved to Bhubaneswar with all my **bags and baggage**. Initially, I stayed at a relative's place. Our classes were to begin soon.*

Then came the most awaited day, ***my real first day, the first class*** *of college.*

I woke up early, finished my chores, and dressed in formal attire: ***black trousers and a white shirt****, the unofficial uniform of engineering life. After a quick bite, I left for the bus stop.*

I noticed a few other students waiting too, but I was too shy to talk to anyone. My heart was pounding.

Suddenly, the ***college bus arrived****.*

It was packed! No place to sit. Seniors occupied all the seats, and the ***freshers stood nervously****, clutching their bags.*

Then came the inevitable:

"Everyone! CLOSE YOUR COLLAR BUTTONS!" *Someone shouted from the back.*

It was my first command from the seniors.

"There were girls in the bus too," I thought. "Do they also have collar buttons as girls used to wear salwar's those days? How stupid is this demand?"

Still, I silently obeyed, closing my collar button and standing stiff like a soldier at a parade.

I didn't dare move. Neither did the other freshers. It felt like we were the passengers of a hijacked bus, ***terrorized by playful terrorists****, the seniors.*

I prayed silently, "Please God, let me get through today safely."

I was drenched in nervous sweat.

Then suddenly, a gentle tap on my shoulder.

I turned, startled, fearing I'd been singled out.

But it was another ***fresher****.*

"Where are you from?" *he asked.*

"Bhadrak district," *I replied quickly.*

"You?"

"Balasore," *he said with a smile.*

My anxiety eased a little. Balasore and Bhadrak were neighboring districts. I had just found my ***first friend in college****; his name was* ***Narendra****.*

The bond we formed in that moment was like finding water in a desert. My nerves calmed instantly.

Thankfully, no senior targeted us on that ride. Soon, the bus reached the ***college campus****.*

As we got off, we were welcomed by ***shouts of slogans****:*

"Vande Mataram!" "Bharat Mata Ki Jai!" (India's Patriotic Slogans)

I was puzzled.

"What's going on? It's neither Independence Day nor Republic Day!"

Before I could gather my thoughts, someone outside shouted,
"Everyone! Form a line!"

There was no choice, we followed like obedient soldiers.

Then came the next order:

"Hold your drawing drafters high and shout 'Vande Mataram!'"

With both hands raised and confusion in our eyes, we chanted loudly, waving our drafters like flags. It was some strange, ***nationalist-style ragging ritual****, a "grand welcome" of sorts for the freshers.*

Finally, we reached our classroom and settled down.

I whispered to myself:

"Don't panic. Life is full of surprises. What starts off scary might turn out to be something beautiful. Just stay cool and go with the flow."

As the days passed, classes began and we were divided into sections—A, B, C, D mixed with students from various branches like Electrical, Mechanical, Electronics, etc. I was in **Section D**.

And that's where I found my ***tribe***.

We were four close friends:

Santosh, Sandeep, Satyajit, and me. *All from* **Electrical Engineering**.

Santosh *was the outspoken one. Having studied in a CBSE school, his English was fluent. He would confidently speak in class, even when his answers were wrong, perhaps to impress the girls. Sadly, his over-enthusiasm didn't win hearts. He wasn't particularly handsome, but he was* **genuine and loyal**. *A true friend.*

Sandeep *was daring but painfully skinny. We called him* **"Nara Kankala"** *which literally means just bones without flesh. But he had a brilliant mathematical mind. His skills with numbers were nothing short of* ***"Math-e-Magics."***

Satyajit *was the calm one. Handsome, but his face was marked by pimples. He was quiet, shy, and rarely spoke to girls. Always well-dressed, always modest.*

And me?

Well… I'll let you decide that by the end of the story.
□

— "Opportunity looks ordinary until courage gives it a shape. Walk into new rooms with humility and hope talent often hides in the quietest corners. Give space to the shy; a single chance can change a lifetime."

2

A Bond Beyond Words

It was the chemistry lab, where all of us from Section D were rearranged into groups of four. My group consisted of ***me, Santosh, Satyajit, and Subhadra****.*

Oh, wait! Before I go any further, let me tell you a bit about Subhadra...

She was a sweet, simple girl from Electrical Engineering, our branch. The first time I saw her standing near the lab table, I was stunned.

As I watched her, I noticed almost by chance, someone across the lab briefly watching us and then looking away. It was nothing at the time, but I filed that face away like an unsent letter, certain later that even the small observers in life sometimes mattered more than we think.

How could someone look so cute, disciplined, and elegant at the same time? Her face was radiant, soft, cream-white, and glowing with a kind of peace I'd never seen in anyone before. Just looking at her could make you forget all your problems. She carried a kind of transparent honesty that reflected in everything she did, like looking through a pane of spotless glass.

You can probably imagine, if she really was like that, how could I not get drawn towards her? And to my luck, she was in **my group**.

That day, we had a 'titration' experiment to perform. Santosh, as usual, tried to initiate conversation with Subhadra while fiddling with lab equipment. I stayed busy focusing on the experiment, and Satyajit, being shy, kept pulling Santosh back towards him to avoid the interaction.

During the experiment, we had to use pipettes and burettes and draw chemicals using our mouths.

Suddenly, Subhadra looked at me and asked sweetly, ***"Can you please draw this for me? I'm unable to do it."***

Inside, I was jumping with joy! But on the outside, I tried to act calm and composed, hiding my excitement. ***"Yes, of course. Give it to me,"*** *I replied.*

I took her pipette and helped with the experiment. That moment was unforgettable. My heart was dancing. I felt like saying, "Dil garden garden ho gaya!" (My heart is blooming like a garden!) because until then, I had never even spoken to a girl due to my shyness. But here she was asking for my help!

After the lab, as we stepped outside, my friends Santosh and Satyajit started teasing me.

"Oye! Congrats! You scored today, bro! Treat dena padega (must give treat)!" *Santosh shouted with laughter.*
"She likes you! She asked you for help, even though we were all there. There's something going on, man. Keep it up!"

They kept teasing, and honestly, their playful banter gave me a little spark of confidence, even though I kept denying everything.

"Come on, yaar. You guys are imagining things," *I replied with a nervous smile.*

But deep down... yes, something was happening.

There was a certain curiosity growing inside me. I started feeling like I wanted to talk to her more... to hear her thoughts... to share mine. I didn't know what I was feeling exactly whether it was love or something else but the desire to be near her was undeniable.

What truly drew me toward her wasn't just her beauty. It was her ***innocence****.*

She never hurt anyone. She talked to everyone kindly, whether it was a boy or a girl. There was no ego, no hesitation. That kind of natural warmth is rare especially among college students, where egos often dominate first impressions. But she was different.

As time passed, we began discussing more during lab sessions, mostly about assignments, records, or practical topics. But never outside. I was still too shy to approach her casually when she was with her friends.

Then came the ***"dark room" physics experiment****, which would change everything.*

Due to the nature of the experiment, our group was split into pairs. And guess what?

She and I were paired together.

I was over the moon.

That entire day, I was lost in thoughts, fantasizing about how the experiment would go, how she'd talk to me, how I'd try to act confident and smart. I couldn't wait.

Just before the lab, I sat at my bench with my head on my bag, pretending to sleep. I told Santosh,

"I'm not feeling well. Wake me up before class."

But I wasn't sleeping. I was wide awake, daydreaming about the upcoming lab.

Finally, Santosh woke me up, and we headed to the dark room. She was already there, punctual as always. We entered the small, dim room together.

She spoke first,

"Subhransu, what do we have to do in this experiment?"

I replied,

"Honestly, I don't know. I think it's about black-body radiation or something. Let's wait for the instructor."

After a few moments of silence, she asked again, ***"How long do we have to wait like this?"***

She was clearly eager to get started, and I admired her focus. To keep the conversation going, I decided to ask her a few things.

"Where do you stay?"

"Aiginia, near Khandagiri," *she replied.*

I chuckled, ***"That's such a funny place name, Aiginia!"*** *She laughed along, and in that moment, the barrier of awkwardness between us shattered.*

We both became more comfortable, and I continued, ***"What does your father do?"***

"He works in the State Secretariat," *she said proudly.*
"Any siblings?"

"One sister and one brother."

Just then, the lab instructor, a rather large, grumpy man stormed into the room.

"Have you started writing anything yet?" *he barked.*

"No sir, we were waiting for instructions," *we said.*

My beautiful moment was interrupted. I felt a bit disappointed. Things were going so well. I was about to show her how sincere, honest, and thoughtful I could be. I wanted her to feel that I genuinely cared.

She must've sensed my sudden shift in mood because she asked,
"What's wrong? Why do you look upset?"

"No, nothing," *I said, pretending to focus on the experiment.*

We finished the practical and met briefly outside the lab to share some notes and discuss the assignment submission. After that, she left with her friends, as she always did.

But that moment in the dark room stayed with me.

Even when I got home that evening, I couldn't stop thinking about it, about her.

Her voice, her smile, the way she spoke with such ease... it all replayed in my head like a movie. I tried to sleep, but every time I closed my eyes, her face appeared.

She was becoming an inseparable part of my thoughts and my life.

That night, after thinking about her all evening, I decided to write something.

Not an assignment. Not a lab report.

Something different.

I pulled out my notebook and wrote a small poem for the very first time in my life. I had never written anything like that before. But that day, it just flowed. The words came from somewhere deep inside, like a whisper from the heart.

It went something like this:

In the dark room, I saw the light,

Not from the lamp, but from your smile so bright.

You asked, "What's wrong?" and I said, "Nothing."

But little did you know, you had started everything.

The next day, I didn't have the courage to give it to her. I tucked it inside my notebook. Hidden. Secret. But as fate would have it, life had a strange plan.

During the afternoon session, our class was asked to submit record books for internal evaluation. In a hurry, I grabbed the wrong notebook, yes, the one with the poem inside and gave it along with the record.

By the time I realized my mistake, it was too late.

Our physics teacher, known for his curiosity, found the poem while checking the records. And instead of keeping it to himself, he read it out loudly in front of the whole class!

"Oh ho! Look what I've found here!" he chuckled, holding the notebook like a prized possession.

My face turned red. My heart was pounding so loudly, I could hear it echoing in my ears.

As he read the lines, a silence fell over the classroom.

Then came the giggles. Then the whistles. And finally, the storm of teasing.

"Waah, poet babu!"

"Arrey Subhransu, scientist or Shakespeare?"

"Who's the lucky girl, huh?"

I was frozen in my seat. Embarrassed. Terrified.

And then… she looked at me.

Subhadra. Her expression wasn't one of anger or embarrassment. She simply smiled.

A slow, warm, understanding smile.

No one knew what that smile meant.

But I did.

Later that day, while leaving college, she walked up beside me, away from the crowd and whispered softly,

"I read it."

My heart skipped a beat.

She continued, "It was beautiful… And no one's ever written something like that for me."

I couldn't say anything. My voice had taken a leave of absence.

She didn't wait for a reply. She just smiled again and walked away, her dupatta flowing behind like a flag of victory.

From that day on, something changed. We still talked like before but now, our conversations had something unspoken in between.

A secret space where words weren't needed.

A place where our hearts had started speaking.

3

The First Fall

After that day, a big change came over me as if I had started a new life. Suddenly, the world looked more beautiful. I began enjoying music, especially romantic songs from the 80s and 90s. I started respecting girls more, and I stopped my friends whenever they made silly comments about them.

But the biggest change was in my everyday behavior. I became more punctual, more disciplined. I took extra care of my appearance, especially in the mornings before college. Every day, I would iron my shirt and pants even if they were already pressed. I thought, "What if she sees me looking clumsy or unkempt? What would she think of me?"

So, I made sure I always looked neat and formal. It became my routine. I didn't even feel like myself anymore, I had transformed.

At the time, I was also a little crazy about everything. Once I committed to something, I would give it my all, physically, mentally, emotionally. That was the intensity I carried within me. I never liked nonsense, and I never passed casual remarks about girls. I was always focused on my studies and sensitive to criticism.

One morning, we were sitting on the department steps, Me, Subhadra, Sangita, Tanushree, and another friend from Electrical Engineering.

Oh wait, I forgot to describe **Sangita and Tanushree***!*

Sangita *was beautiful and bold. She lived near Ravi Talkies, the same area where I stayed. Since her house was close to a big municipal water tank, we jokingly called her* **"Pani-Tanki"** *(Water Tank Girl). She hated that nickname, but it stuck. She was smart, outspoken, and always well-dressed. Most people were a little scared of her because she would lash out publicly if anyone made a mistake, no filters, no second chances. But deep down, she was kind and knowledgeable.*

Tanushree*, on the other hand, was the complete opposite. Simple, soft-spoken, and reserved. She rarely engaged in banter or gossip.*

That day, as we sat on the steps, Subhadra turned to me and asked softly,

"Can you do me a favor?"

"Of course," *I replied.*

"Tanushree is hungry. Can you get her some vegetable patties from the canteen?"

I nodded and went immediately.

She offered me money, but I refused to take it. I went to the canteen, ordered the patties, and sat on a bench while I waited.

That's when it hit me. A wave of emotions crashed over me, and I broke down.

I had never taken orders from anyone before. I felt like I was being used like a messenger or an errand boy. The thought that girls might be using boys like this really hurt my ego.

I wasn't angry because of the request itself. I could have happily done it if it were an emergency. But this felt unnecessary. They could've gone themselves.

I felt deeply insulted. But more than that, I was afraid. Afraid that if I said something, even by mistake, it might damage the fragile connection I had just begun to build with Subhadra.

So, I swallowed my pride and emotions, returned with the patties, and quietly handed them over. She didn't even ask me to stay. She just said, ***"Thank you."***

That made it worse.

My reactive and sensitive nature got the better of me. I kept thinking, "If a boy had done this to me, I would've started a full-blown fight. But because it's her… I'm just accepting it?"

Still, I didn't show any of this to her. She had no idea that I was hurt. Days passed, and I continued to be a good friend to her. My attachment to her only grew stronger.

One day, while walking home with Santosh and Sandeep, we started talking about college, friends, hostel life and somehow, the conversation turned to Subhadra.

Santosh said, ***"She likes you."***

I shrugged.

"I don't know. I never thought of it like that. She's a good friend, and yes, she seems more comfortable with me than with others… but that's it."

Sandeep jumped in. ***"Why don't you propose to her? Let's see what happens!"***

Then he paused and added, ***"Actually… wait. I've got a better idea."***

I was curious. ***"What? What's the idea?"***

Sandeep leaned in like a movie villain plotting something wild.
"Okay, listen. You stay absent from college for a few days. Don't tell her anything. Since she's your lab partner, she'll ask us about you."

Santosh and I nodded, listening.

"Then we'll tell her… you've been diagnosed with cancer. Doctors say you've only got a year to live. We'll tell her you were asking for her in the hospital. That you confessed your love. That you said you can't live without her… that your dying wish is to see her accept your love."

We all burst out laughing.

"Kya planning hai bhai! (What a Planning!) You're a mastermind!" *I said, half-amused and half-horrified.*

But soon, the laughter faded. I looked at Sandeep and said seriously,
"No, yaar. I don't want to lie to her or create such drama. If she accepts me, I want it to be because of who I am not because I fooled her with sympathy."

Truth is a small, powerful currency. Spend it wisely.

I paused, then added,

"I believe in truth. In honesty. If she's meant to be mine, I'll win her over with my behavior, not tricks. I'm not looking for some short-term fling or one-sided story."

That idea felt dangerous even then, not because of the lie, but because it showed how easily we could manufacture sympathy. I promised myself I'd never weaponize truth or pity. Later, I'd understand how fragile trust can be.

Sandeep smirked.

"You're too innocent, Subhransu. But remember, our feelings, our hormones, will drive us to do anything when we're really in love. One day, you'll be desperate to make her yours. You'll become restless. And when that happens… you'll remember what I said today."

He laughed and walked ahead.

We all reached our locality and said goodbye for the day.

But his words stuck in my mind, haunting me more than I expected.

— *"Honesty is the simplest form of strength. Do not trade truth for a short gain of sympathy or spectacle. Live with integrity, your reputation and relationships will repay you far beyond any momentary drama."*

4

Signals of the Soul

As the days passed, I couldn't help but notice how Santosh kept trying to impress the girls. He always tried to talk more to Subhadra, joking, flirting, laughing a little too loudly whenever she was around. And I... well, I couldn't stand it.

Out of jealousy, I often found myself trying to divert his attention or pull him away from her. I never made it obvious, but deep down, I was possessive. I didn't even realize how gradually, and unknowingly, I had started to care for her.

At least when it came to academics, I was always there for her offering help whenever she needed it. Whether it was a lab assignment submission, technical questions, lending a book, or just helping her understand something, I was always mentally prepared to support her.

I felt truly happy to have a friend like her. And yes, she was becoming increasingly beautiful in my eyes with each passing day.

One of the most important things I forgot to mention, **we had started talking on the phone regularly.** *She had shared her landline number with me during one of our Physics lab sessions:*

0674–2600152.
It was a WLL (Wireless in Local Loop) number.

During those phone calls, we had some deep conversations.

She often shared details about her family. Most of the time, she seemed upset with her mother. Subhadra believed her mother had changed with time. She often said, "During school days, Maa (Her Mother) used to talk about selflessness, helping others, doing something for the nation. But now she just seems irritated all the time. She only thinks about the family, not others."

What Subhadra didn't realize was that her mother's behavior had come from love and responsibility, not selfishness. She couldn't distinguish between practical sacrifice and philosophical ideals. She had misunderstood her mother's intentions, seeing them as contradictions.

That's when I felt I should explain things to her, help her understand the emotional dynamics of family and life. I thought, Maybe I can guide her, help her see things differently.

One day, I wrote down a few motivational thoughts and life lessons on a piece of paper and gave it to her. I wrapped it up like a small gift, hoping she wouldn't treat it as just another piece of paper but something valuable that might help her later.

That was the ***first gift I ever gave her****.*

To encourage her morally, to help her understand family values, and to provide clarity about how society and life work. I explained a lot to her over the phone. Bit by bit, I narrated what I had learned through experience. How life tests us. How our responsibilities shape us. And how we often fail to see the sacrifices others make for us—especially parents.

Let me share with you a part of what I told her that night. It was an hour-long call, one of the most heartfelt conversations I've ever had.

"Subhadra, I want to share something very real with you."
She stayed silent, listening.

"Life is like a mountain trek. We keep climbing with energy, expecting to find a beautiful view. But sometimes we get hurt. Sometimes we fall. And often, the view isn't what we imagined, but we still must keep going."

"Your mother isn't against the values she taught you. She's just exhausted. She's doing her part to hold the family together, something you'll only understand when you step into her shoes one day. But until then, try to see the intent behind her actions. Sometimes, love is hidden behind silence. Sometimes, concern comes out as scolding."

She didn't say much, but I could feel she was reflecting on my words.

That phone call changed something between us. I could feel a shift. She started seeing me not just as a friend or a classmate, but as someone who genuinely cared for her, someone who wanted her to grow.

After that, she slowly started talking more openly sometimes even about personal things.

We never explicitly said the words, but an emotional bond had started forming between us. It was beyond attraction. It was trust.

And that trust... was becoming the foundation of everything we were yet to face.

A few days after that heartfelt phone conversation with Subhadra, something strange happened, something that even today sends a chill down my spine whenever I think about it.

It was a regular weekday morning. I reached college early and as usual, went straight to the classroom. Only a few students had arrived, so the room was mostly empty. I placed my bag on the desk, sat down, and pulled out my notebook.

That's when I noticed it.

A small, folded piece of paper was tucked inside my notebook neatly folded and sealed with tape.

At first, I thought it was one of those silly prank notes we often exchanged in class. But this was different. It had no name, no handwriting I could recognize, no signs of a joke.

The front of the paper simply had one word ***"Read."***

Sometimes a nameless recognition sustains a person more than praise; notice the unnoticed.

That unsigned note felt like a message from outside my life, a mirror reflecting what I dared not say. For days afterward I kept glancing at that folded paper in my mind; it was a quiet reminder that someone else had read my heart before I even knew how to write it.

I carefully peeled off the tape, unfolded the letter, and started reading.

"You talk like a philosopher. You listen like a friend. You care like a brother. But I've seen your eyes, Subhransu... they hide more than words ever can.

I don't know if you've noticed, but someone watches how you talk to her. Someone has seen how you wait for her outside the lab, how you skip your lunch just to help her with notes, how you iron your shirt twice because you think she might see you.

She doesn't see it. But I do.

And maybe someday, she will too.

You may not be a hero. But the way you care... is not ordinary.

Keep walking. Don't change.

From someone who sees."

I was frozen.

My eyes kept reading the lines repeatedly.

It felt like someone had written what I had never dared to say out loud. Someone had read my heart like an open book. But who?

I looked around. The room was still half-empty. Nobody was watching. No unusual expressions. No giggles. Nothing.

That letter didn't carry a name, but it carried something far deeper, a recognition. A silent salute from someone who saw what I never intended to show.

For a few seconds, I couldn't breathe. I felt like the world had paused. Everything around me blurred. I just sat there... still... stunned.

Later that evening, I went to the hostel rooftop and sat alone. The sunset spread golden light across the sky, but inside me, there was a storm.

Was it from her? Was it from a friend? Or... was it from someone else entirely? I never found out. But from that day on, something shifted inside me.

I realized that when your love is true even if unspoken, **someone, somewhere, always sees.**

And sometimes... that's enough to keep you going.

— *"Someone sees your quiet care even before you say it, let that recognition steady you. Choose small, steady kindness over loud gestures, consistent care changes lives. Understand the sacrifices behind others' actions, compassion begins with listening. Keep walking with integrity: patience, truth and humility build lasting love."*

5

When Silence Speaks

Almost 4 months later'...

I shifted from my relative's home to a private hostel as my semester exams were nearing. I thought I'd be able to concentrate better there, less distraction, more discipline. At least, that was the plan.

We were three; Narendra, Subrat, and me sharing a room with two of our super seniors, final-year Computer Science students who happened to be Narendra's relatives. Though Subrat and Narendra were from the Electronics branch, we had met during our first semester through mixed group classes and quickly became friends.

And just as I was trying to settle in, life had other plans. My father's heart condition worsened again. He already had a history of heart disease and was living with a permanent electronic pacemaker implanted to regulate his heartbeat; quite literally, a machine keeping him alive.

One evening, I got a frantic call from my mother. Her voice was shaking; panic and helplessness were spilling through the phone. The pacemaker had become exposed due to an infection and had stopped working. My father, being entirely dependent on that device, needed immediate surgery. And not just anywhere, we had to take him all the way to SSSIHMS, Bangalore, the hospital where he had undergone his previous operation.

I didn't think twice. I packed up, rushed home, and started planning the journey to Bangalore.

Being the only responsible son in a family of eight (with four elder sisters and one younger brother), the weight of the situation fell squarely on my shoulders. I was the fourth child but the only son old enough to handle things. My father, a humble high school clerk, earned just ₹7000 a month, yes, that was it. And yet, with unmatched courage and relentless sacrifice, he gave us everything: education, stability, and a sense of dignity.

With no fancy house or overflowing bank account, he taught us something far more valuable, self-confidence and the power of education. He would often say, "If my children are educated and settled, that will be my true achievement, not a bungalow, not a bank balance." And true to his words, he poured every ounce of himself into nurturing us.

Looking back, it's his sacrifices that allowed us to stand with our heads held high today. Without him, God knows where we might've ended up.

When I was in Class 7, in 1994, my father suffered a massive heart attack. He became frail after that and remained under strict medical care ever since. I was just 12 years old. My sisters were too young to understand the world, and my baby brother was, well… just a baby.

At that point, my mother stepped up like a warrior. She managed the hospital visits, the household, the children, everything. Our financial liabilities quickly spiraled to around ₹3–4 lakhs. For a middle-class family living on ₹7000 a month and raising six children, one of whom was a heart patient; this was nothing short of a nightmare. We borrowed money from relatives, friends, anyone who would help.

To make matters worse, my elder sisters couldn't contribute anything to the household. After completing their graduation, they neither found work nor pursued anything independently. It worsened our situation and added fuel to the fire of our financial crisis.

I became my parents' only hope, the one they believed would rise, earn well, repay the debts, ensure my sisters' marriages, and support my younger brother's education.

We didn't even have a home of our own. Due to years of misunderstandings and unfair treatment from my father's family, especially his elder brother, my parents left their ancestral home when I was just five months. They decided to stand on their own feet and raise their children with dignity, no matter what.

They fought life tooth and nail to build a future for us.

But fate is rarely fair. As the saying goes, "Man proposes, God disposes." That held true for my parents too. In a society still caught up in superstitions and gender biases, they also became victims of the belief that having a son would secure their future. After three daughters, they kept hoping for a son and ended up with six children: four girls and two boys.

With every child, our financial burdens grew heavier. We eventually had to sell our only house and a small piece of land to pay for my elder sister's wedding. After that, we moved into a government quarter allotted to my father; just one room, 10ft x 12ft, with an asbestos roof and no attached toilet. The toilet was outside, and our only source of water was a tube well half a kilometer away.

That tiny room, with its leaking roof and shared walls, was home for ten long years.

On one side, my father was battling a life-threatening heart condition. His treatment costs loomed large. On the other, my sisters had reached the age of marriage, yet we lacked even a decent home to live in. My younger brother and sister still had years of education ahead of them. I, too, was still a student.

All of this, our growing financial burden, my father's deteriorating health, incomplete education, and the absence of a stable home, pushed us into a deep, suffocating struggle for survival. Sustainability wasn't just a challenge; it was a daily question of existence.

I vividly remember how we stretched every single day to meet our basic needs. There were times when our meals consisted of nothing more than plain rice, or just dal, or a small helping of local fried vegetables. On good days, if we managed to afford two vegetables and some rice, we rationed it. Day one, just rice. Day two, rice with one vegetable. Day three, the second one. This is how we survived: by making the most of the least.

By the time I reached Class 12, I was fully aware of our condition and of my purpose. I knew exactly why I had been born into that family, in that moment of time. I was mentally prepared and determined to rise above it all. I wanted to earn enough to resolve every single problem my family faced. Most of all, I wanted to restore the dignity my parents had lost the day they walked out of their ancestral home, cut off from my father's elder brother and the rest of the family, forced to start a new from nothing.

I was deeply driven to change not just our situation, but to bring reform, real change to the society around me. I dreamed of earning enough to clear our debts, secure my siblings' future, and provide proper treatment for my father so he could live without pain.

But back then, I had very little clarity about higher education, what it was, how it worked, what to pursue, or even how to dream big. Neither my parents nor my sisters had any idea about the education system or how to build a life beyond it. In my village, if someone passed matriculation with a first division, they were hailed as a bright student regardless of the percentage.

Because of our financial situation, I couldn't get into a well-reputed school. I had to settle for a private school with limited resources and minimal academic value. Even the tuition classes I attended weren't exceptional, but they were enough to help me clear the matriculation exam with a first division. Without that help, even that might've been out of reach. I still respect and thank my tutor for doing whatever he could within his means to help me.

I grew up in a tiny village called Ghanteswar, in Bhadrak district, a place where awareness struggled to reach. Due to the lack of exposure and proper guidance, I had little idea about quality education, competitive scoring, or future career paths. Up until my 10th *standard, all I knew was: If I score a first division, I'll have a chance to do something in life. But even then, I didn't know that it wasn't just about passing, it was about percentage. I used to believe that high marks were something only students from government or reputed schools could achieve.*

Despite all that, I managed to secure a first division and even topped my school. That alone was enough for my father to allow me into the Science stream. He had a simple rule: Any child who secured a first division in

Class 10, son or daughter, could study Science. The rest had to take Arts.

I didn't have proper guidance. But one thing I always had without fail, was my parents' belief in me. They may not have known the technicalities of education, but they gave me courage, faith, and relentless support. They always said, "No matter how hard life gets, if your heart is in it, nothing is impossible."

And today, I can honestly say: they gave me everything they had. Everything they knew. Everything they understood. That, to me, was everything.

If I failed to explore more or learn beyond what was around me, it wasn't because of them, it was due to the severe lack of awareness, isolation from the right kind of society, and a family mindset that often leaned toward bias in decisions. Up to my 10th standard, I remained mostly disconnected from any peer group or support system that could have helped me grow.

That, more than anything else, was the reason my development felt stunted in those early years.

After passing Class 12, I secured admission to Bhadrak Autonomous College, one of the more reputed institutions in Bhadrak district. I enrolled in a Bachelor of Science program with Automobile as my major, alongside Physics and Mathematics (PMAM). For a while, it felt like I was finally walking down a steady academic path.

But one year into the course, I had a moment of reckoning.

By then, I had matured. I understood the weight of my responsibilities and the urgency of my family's situation. Continuing B.Sc. in the same manner, without a clear direction, felt like walking in circles. I needed to do something different, something that would strengthen my credentials, give me a respectable career, and most importantly, create a sustainable future for my family.

One day, without waiting to appear for the first-year exams, I packed my bags and moved to Balasore, Odisha (The one famous for Medical Coaching in that area). I had made up my mind: I wanted to prepare for the Medical Entrance Examination. Becoming a doctor, I thought, would not only give me the financial stability we so desperately needed but also restore my parents' lost dignity within the extended family.

So, I began preparing for the medical entrance. But coaching classes were expensive, and with no financial support, I couldn't afford them. I had to prepare on my own. To sustain myself, I started giving part-time tuitions to students up to Class 10.

It was the year 2000 when I first appeared for the Odisha Joint Entrance Examination (OJEE) for both Engineering and Medical streams. The results were a mixed bag: I didn't qualify in Medical, but I did manage to secure a rank of 8291 in Engineering.

That result opened my eyes. I realized that medical wasn't my strong suit, Biology was not my friend. I saw brilliant students who had been trying for 2–3 years and still hadn't cleared the medical entrance. Competition was fierce, with very few government seats and thousands of aspirants each year.

I knew I didn't have the luxury of time. My family needed me to step up now. So, I dropped the idea of medical altogether and chose to focus on engineering. It seemed more practical and achievable, and it could offer quicker job prospects.

Every decision I took during that time, I took alone.

There was no one to guide me. My family lacked knowledge about higher education. Even our relatives were clueless. Whatever clarity I gained was through my growing network of friends, exposure to society, and slowly piecing things together myself. I joined a coaching center and continued giving private tuitions to manage my expenses.

The next year, I appeared for the entrance again, this time focusing only on engineering, and secured a better rank: ***5051*** *in the entire state. It was a relief, but not enough. That rank wouldn't get me a free seat. A paid seat was too costly, and we had no idea where the money would come from. Still, I didn't lose hope.*

I decided to give it one more shot.

I couldn't afford coaching this time, so I prepared on my own. I revisited all my Class 12 lessons, focused on clearing my concepts, and gave everything I had. I hoped this time I'd finally secure a good enough rank for a 'free seat' something I could act on.

But fate had other plans.

Just days before the entrance exam, my father's condition took a sharp turn for the worse. Doctors diagnosed him with Complete Heart Block (CHB). It was serious, his heart was no longer responding to medication. The only way to save him was through immediate implantation of a pacemaker.

This was the first time we truly understood how critical his condition had become. Back in my Class 7 days, when he had his first heart attack, doctors had assured us that medication would be enough. And for years, it seemed to work. But now, that option had expired. Surgery was the only way forward.

We were financially broken, burdened with loans and surviving on borrowed time and hope. But we gathered our courage, borrowed money again, and rushed him to Sri Sathya Sai Institute of Higher Medical Sciences (SSSIHMS), Whitefield, Bangalore. It was a charity hospital that provided all treatment free of cost. We only had to cover our travel and stay which still cost us around ₹30,000, all borrowed.

Thankfully, the surgery was successful. My father recovered. We returned home after 15 nerve-wracking days, right before my entrance exam.

But those 15 days cost me my preparation. I couldn't revise, couldn't even open a book. My mind was blank. Still, I appeared for the exam, relying on whatever I could remember from the past year. But deep down, I already knew, I hadn't done enough. Again, disappointment crept in.

This time, it felt heavier.

Years were slipping by. Since finishing Class 12, nearly ***three years*** *had gone without any tangible progress. One year wasted in B.Sc., two more in preparation. My career had a massive gap. Time was moving, and I felt stuck.*

At home, the pressure was building. My mother, who had always been my emotional anchor, was beginning to lose her calm. She broke down and said, "Your father's health is fragile. He's dependent on a pacemaker now, and it must be replaced every five years, maybe even sooner if it malfunctions. And your sisters need to get married too. We can't wait anymore. You must do something."

Her words hit me hard. She wasn't blaming me, just desperate. She had pinned all her hopes on me, and I had nothing concrete to show.

I held her hands and said, "Just give me a little more time. Let me get into engineering. I promise within the next 4–5 years, things will change."

That promise wasn't just to her; it was to me. I had to make it work. Not just for me, but for all of us.

*A few days later, my entrance exam result was declared. My rank was **2244**. Not exceptional, but decent enough to get me a **free seat** (read: reduced tuition, not entirely free) in a reputable engineering college. I knew I couldn't afford to wait another year. Time was slipping, and my family couldn't bear the burden any longer. I had to take admission now.*

*Thankfully, my cousin brother and uncle stepped in to support me. They encouraged me to opt for **Electrical Engineering** and suggested a well-known college in Bhubaneswar, **C.V. Raman College of Engineering**, where I could secure a free seat.*

*That hurdle seemed crossed, but the real mountain was still in front of me, **the admission fee**.*

We didn't have a single rupee. Just weeks earlier, we had borrowed ₹30,000 for my father's pacemaker surgery. My father had already taken loans for our education, daily expenses, and survival. Creditors began knocking at our door daily, some harsh, some humiliating. The idea of arranging even a minimal amount for admission felt impossible.

*I still remember that day vividly. My sister handed me a pair of her gold earrings, the only significant ornament she had and we set out early in the morning. From **6 AM to 9 PM**, we wandered from door to door, looking for someone willing to accept the gold as collateral and lend us money. After an exhausting day, we finally succeeded. I secured just enough to cover the admission.*

But I knew, I would have to return that money, with interest. Every borrowed rupee felt like a new promise I had to fulfil.

*Once admission was done, I started approaching banks for an **education loan**. But every door closed on me. My academic percentages in 10th and 12th weren't high enough. One **SBI branch manager** did offer a condition:*

*"Secure **80%** in your first semester, and then I'll approve your loan."*

I nodded politely, but inside I was crushed. What if I fail to meet the target? What then? How will I study for four years? How will I clear our debts? Support my family? Get my sisters married? Fund my father's future treatments?

The weight of these questions was too much. That evening, I broke down in front of my mother. I cried like a child. She sat beside me, wrapped her arms around my trembling shoulders, and gently said:

"Don't worry, beta (Son). God is watching. Do your part with full heart. He will take care of the rest."

That moment changed something in me. Her words didn't just console me, they ignited me.

I returned to Bhubaneswar, fired up with a mission: No matter what, I will score 80%. I immersed myself in my studies like never before. Day and night, I worked relentlessly, determined to prove myself to the bank, to the world, and to the mirror.

By then, I had also met ***Subhadra****, and slowly, silently, I had started liking her. But even with that budding feeling in the background, my mind remained razor-focused: Get that loan. Finish engineering. Get a job. Rescue my family.*

That was the only dream I had ever dared to dream.

I never wished for riches, fame, or luxury. My only aim was to stabilize my family, nothing more. In a way, it felt like I was born with that singular purpose. And I carried it with pride. I never saw it as a burden. It was simply mine.

But as the saying goes, ***"Man proposes, God disposes."***

Just when everything was falling into place, life struck again.

Fifteen days before my semester exams, my father's pacemaker developed an infection. After a brief call with the doctors, we were told to rush him back to ***Bangalore****. We borrowed whatever we could and made our way to* ***SSSIHMS****, Whitefield. My mother and I were the only ones by his side.*

Five days before the exam, the doctors confirmed the infection was serious, and surgery was scheduled immediately. That meant I had to decide, stay back for the operation, or return to Bhubaneswar to appear for the exam that would decide my loan, and my future.

I was torn.

If I stayed, my mother would be alone during the surgery, and anything could happen. But if I left, I would miss my chance to secure that loan. Flight tickets were out of the question. Train travel would take 30 hours minimum, sometimes more. Every option felt like a lose-lose.

When my father sensed I was considering skipping the exam, he became visibly stressed. My mother took me aside and said, firmly:

"Go. Book your ticket and appear for the exam. I'll handle everything here."

Her confidence was the strength I needed.

So, with a heart heavier than ever before, I left Bangalore and reached Bhubaneswar just a day before the exam. I hadn't revised anything in 15 days. Everything I had studied seemed to fade away. My father's face on the hospital bed haunted me. My mother's anxious eyes flashed before me. My notebooks were damp with tears.

But I had to try.

I stayed up all night, skimming through chapters, hoping to retain just enough. I prayed, "God, please help me survive this."

I appeared for the exam, then studied between gaps for the rest of the papers. I gave it everything I could under those circumstances. But I knew, it probably wasn't enough for 80%. Doubts crept in. The fear of failure returned. Yet, somewhere deep inside, I held on to faith.

Meanwhile, my father's surgery was successful. He was discharged, and they returned home safely. And just before my result was declared, **miraculously**, *I got an education loan* ***from a different bank****, thanks to one of my father's personal connections.*

That day, I learned one of life's most important lessons:

"Don't overthink the future. Do what the moment demands. Leave the rest to God."

When I chose to prioritize my father over my exam, I didn't know what would happen next. But somehow, the universe aligned. The exam, the loan, the surgery, everything fell into place. Maybe that's what faith truly means.

After our semester exams ended, summer had arrived and with it came the much-awaited vacation. One by one, students started heading back to their homes. I had also packed my bags and was all set to leave the next morning. Everything was ready, the luggage, the ticket, the excitement of going home. Only a few of us were still left behind, planning to leave the next day.

That evening, after packing up, I sat quietly in the balcony. But something didn't feel right. I couldn't focus, wasn't feeling at peace. A strange restlessness had taken over me. I couldn't quite put my finger on it, but deep inside, it felt like I was leaving something or someone behind. It was around 8 PM when I couldn't take it anymore.

Without thinking twice, I rushed to the nearest ***STD booth*** *and dialed her number.*

"Hello," she answered. I froze for a second. My throat tightened. I didn't know what to say, but I knew I needed to hear her voice.

"Hello…?" she said again. Words began tumbling out of me all at once, in a low, quiet, almost trembling voice. "I don't know why, but I've been feeling uneasy all day. Even though I'm going home, it feels like I'm leaving someone behind. I just… I don't know. I needed to call you."

There was a pause and then came her soft reply, ***"Me too."*** *Something shifted inside me in that moment.*

Then, unexpectedly, her cousin ***Santu*** *grabbed the receiver and chuckled, "Dei wanted to tell you something but couldn't say it!"*

He continued, laughing like he'd just exposed the world's biggest secret. "I heard her talking with Rinky Dei & Pinky Dei (both sisters) wanted to tell you something."

My heart skipped a beat.

A jolt ran through my entire body like an electric current. I couldn't believe what I was hearing.

"What did she want to say?" I asked instantly, my voice almost cracking. In the background, I heard her shout, "Santu! Stop it! Don't say anything!"

But Santu, clearly enjoying his mischief, replied, ***"She wanted to say, 'I love you' to you."*** *And just like that, my entire world tilted.*

For a moment, everything stopped—my thoughts, my breath, my reality. Was this real? Or was I dreaming?

But before I could say anything, she snatched the phone and said in a panic, "Please don't take it seriously! He's just being a fool! He was joking, don't believe him! I'm sorry..."

I tried to play it cool, acting like I hadn't heard anything. "I didn't quite catch what he said," I lied.

"Oh, thank God!" she sighed. "Good. Let it be. He was just fooling around."

I pushed a little more, "No seriously... what did he say?"

She hurriedly responded, "Papa (Her Father) is here, I must go. I'll call you tomorrow around 10:30 AM. Promise!" "Alright," I replied, not hiding my curiosity.

Though I had heard every word loud and clear, I still wanted to hear it from her... I needed to know whether it was real or just a prank. I delayed my journey home, postponing my bus until the afternoon, just so I wouldn't miss her call.

The next morning, I was up by ***5:30 AM****, pacing back and forth like a restless soul. Those five hours felt like five years. I couldn't sit still. I couldn't focus on anything except the upcoming phone call.*

*Finally, around 10:30 AM, the STD booth boy shouted from below our balcony, "****Subhransu! You've got a call!****"*

I rushed downstairs, heart pounding, hands shaking.

"Hello!" I answered eagerly. "Hey, it's Sandeep," came the voice from the other end.

I swear, I felt like a glass shattered somewhere inside my chest.

"Chhh..." slipped out involuntarily as disappointment washed over me. He spoke for a bit about classes and vacation plans, but my mind was elsewhere.

*Just as I stepped out of the booth, the boy shouted again, "**Subhransu! Another call!**"*

My heart jumped. It had to be her. I ran back, picked up the receiver.

*"**Hi, it's Subhadra!** What were you doing?" she asked, casually.*

"Nothing... just waiting for this call," I replied honestly, not wasting a second. "It's already 10:50 AM. Now tell me what yesterday was all about."

She sighed, then said with a careful tone, "Subhransu, we're good friends. Whatever Santu said, it's not true. He's just an idiot. Don't mind him, please. There's nothing like that between us."

I tried to mask my disappointment. "It's okay. I didn't take it seriously," I said, trying to reassure her, though a part of me hoped she'd say something else.

But deep inside, I couldn't shake off those words. I kept wondering: Could Santu have made that up? Really? It felt too specific... too real.

That night, something changed inside me. I started thinking about her differently. The fear I had of expressing my feelings slowly began to melt away. Even though she had denied it, something told me it wasn't entirely untrue.

Later that day, I finally left for home. During the vacation, I barely got the chance to speak with her. Being with family made it difficult, especially with my sharp-eyed elder sister around, she had an uncanny ability to read people and would have surely figured something out.

So, I stayed quiet... but in my heart, something had already begun.

— *"Hold your duty and your dreams together with equal hands, responsibility need not kill hope, it must fuel it. When family calls, answer with courage; when opportunity knocks, meet it with preparation, both matters. Faith is not passive; it's the quiet work you do while trusting the rest to unfold. Carry love gently alongside your duty that balance makes a life steady, not fragile."*

6

Love, Unshaken

My vacation had ended. I returned from home on ***28th May 2003****, sometime around 8 PM. That evening, a firm thought took root in my heart, I had to say it. I couldn't live in this state of silent confusion any longer. So, I rushed to the* ***STD booth****, heart thudding, palms slightly sweaty, and without a second thought, I* ***proposed to her over the phone****.*

There was silence on the other end.

"Hello...? Hello ...?" I repeated, nervous energy bubbling in my voice.

No response.

I was crazy back then, reckless in the most romantic sense of the word. I didn't give her any time to process or even breathe. I blurted it out and waited, already imagining her saying yes. I was anxious, but somewhere inside, I was certain that she'll say yes... she must.

But instead, she replied softly, "See Subhransu, we're good friends. I think we should not step beyond that. Things are fine the way they are. Please try to understand..."

And then came the usual "blah blah blah," just like all the other girls in every love story who try to keep the boat from rocking too much.

But I had gone too far. I was way past the shore, deep into the ocean of emotions. I couldn't let go just like that.

I pleaded, "Please just tell me... do you love me or not? I won't hang up until you answer. Please... don't cut the call... please."

But she was busy helping in the kitchen, and her father was around.

"My father is here. I'll talk to you later. Please try to understand."

I had no choice. I didn't want to push too hard and make things worse. So, I swallowed my desperation and said, "Okay... I won't ask again. But please... tell me later."

And I gently put down the receiver with a soft, "Take care."

But my mind was in absolute chaos.

What had I done? Was I losing my best friend? Would I be able to face her again? Had I misread everything? If she had always seen me as a friend, then was I completely wrong to think there was something more?

That night, a thousand thoughts ran through my head. The confusion, the guilt, the awkwardness, it all crept in and slowly started to change me.

I tried again the next day, hoping to convince her, but the result was the same, nothing changed.

That's when I started withdrawing. Our conversations became fewer. I couldn't bring myself to speak the same way again. I felt awkward, exposed, and unsure of how to even look her in the eye.

I became silent. College became a blur. I walked the corridors like a ghost—quiet, detached, avoiding eye contact. My energy faded, and I kept to myself.

Eventually, she noticed. Despite not accepting my proposal, she didn't want to lose the friendship we shared. She kept asking me why I had become so quiet. But I couldn't answer her, not because I didn't want to, but because I didn't know how to.

That's when **Sangita** *stepped in.*

It was still ***28th May****, and we had a college holiday. I was in my hostel when Sangita called.*

"Come to college. Subhadra is coming too. We need to talk something important."

Without hesitation, I agreed. I had been spiraling anyway. Maybe this was the turning point.

I took an auto to the meeting spot, where both Sangita and Subhadra were waiting. We rode together in silence, well, they talked, I mostly nodded. My thoughts were too loud inside to speak.

We reached college, which was nearly empty except for a few office staff and construction workers. We settled into an open classroom. No one spoke. Subhadra sat there like a shy, innocent child, eyes low, quietly hoping that maybe Sangita could work a miracle and patch things up.

I wanted the same. I really did. But my heart was still tangled.

Finally, Sangita broke the silence.

"Subhransu, say something. How long will we just sit here like this?"

I replied honestly, "I don't know what to say... I really don't. This silence, this distance, it just happened. I didn't plan it. I've come here to listen. If there's something you want to say, please do."

Sangita looked at me with understanding. Then she leaned in, gently, and said:

"Why are you worrying so much? We have three more years of college ahead. This is just the beginning. I understand your feelings and hers too. Keep the friendship strong, and with time, everything will fall into place. One day, she'll say yes. Trust me. She already likes you... but commitment takes time. Be patient. Be normal. Just go back to being friends."

Her words hit me like a splash of cold water, shocking but awakening.

She was right. Why was I in such a rush? This was just the first semester. There was so much time ahead. And more than anything else, I didn't want to lose her, not even as a friend.

Suddenly, I smiled.

I remembered how it all began, the casual chats, the shared jokes, the little glances that meant more than words. I looked at Subhadra and gave her a soft, teasing smile.

She blushed.

Her lips curled into a quiet, adorable smile, her eyes still shy, looking down. Then she glanced up and asked softly, "Is it okay now? From today, we're friends again... like before? Say yes... please?"

Her voice held a blend of hope, apology, and that gentle stubbornness she always carried.

I reached out and gave her a playful pinch on her cheek and said, ***"Okay, baba. Don't worry. I'll be your friend—done, done, done!"***

She turned her face away with a shy grin.

By the time we reached the ***National Highway*** *on our way back, the awkwardness had melted. That day became one of the* ***most unforgettable memories*** *of our early friendship; messy, emotional, real… and beautiful.*

— "Brave confessions are noble but respect the other person's pace; love won by pressure is not love at all. When words create awkward silence, gentle patience and honest listening mend the gap better than pleading. Guard the friendship first; steady care and time often prove truer than a hurried declaration. Be brave enough to speak, humble enough to accept the answer, and wise enough to keep the bond whole."

7

Bound by Us

*It was **23rd June 2003**. We were back to being good friends, just like before. Everything seemed normal on the outside. But inside? My heart refused to calm down. That spark I had once felt for her was still very much alive, and no matter how* **hard** *I tried, I couldn't ignore it.*

*It was around **5 PM**. I was lying on my bed, completely consumed by my thoughts. Why did she say no? Did she not feel anything for me? Or had I just failed to make her understand my feelings? My mind was a complete mess, full of questions that had no answers.*

But I've never been one to give up easily. If I start something, I see it through. I'm not the kind of person who quits halfway and love, this love, was no different.

Driven by that same restless determination, I sprang from my bed and rushed to the nearby ***cybercafé/STD booth****. I called her again. But this time, fate had other plans, her father answered. She wasn't home.*

I sighed, said, "Okay, I'll call later," and hung up.

Later that night, with even more desperation in my voice, I called again. She picked up.

"Hello?" she said, sensing something off.

"Hey," I replied, my voice low. "How are you?"

She paused. "What happened, Subhransu? You sound... upset. Is everything okay?"

"I'm fine," I lied. "I tried calling you earlier. You weren't home."

"I had gone out. What was it? Something important?"

I didn't waste any more time.

"Please say yes, just once. Why are you so reluctant? What's stopping you?"

She hesitated, then gave me the same reply as before. "We're friends, Subhransu. And we're great that way. Why spoil it? Please try to understand. Focus on your studies. Let's keep everything normal."

But I wasn't ready to hear any of that.

I quietly put down the receiver and just sat there in the booth, heart heavy, eyes misty. I eventually walked back to my room and collapsed on the bed, tears silently slipping down.

Her words kept echoing in my mind, "We're just friends, try to understand..." But I couldn't. I simply couldn't.

Her presence had already become a part of me. Talking to her felt like breathing. I was living in a dream world where time flew whenever I spoke with her. I was sinking deeper into her love and there was no coming back.

The hardest part was knowing she liked me, cared for me, but just didn't want to love me. She kept insisting, "I'm not the right girl for you. You'll find someone better." That confused me even more. Was she hiding something? Was she in love with someone else? But unless she said it out loud, I'd never know.

Still, one thing was clear: I didn't want her by force, I wanted her by choice, her choice.

But my heart wasn't ready to give up.

The next day, ***24th June 2003****, I called her again.*

And this time, I was dead serious.

"If you don't say yes today, I'm not hanging up. I'll stay in this booth until you do. Let the bill run into lakhs. I won't eat. I won't sleep. I won't move. But I won't disconnect until I hear that one word."

She fell silent. I could feel her dilemma through the silence.

She was torn, if she said no, she feared losing our friendship. But if she said yes, she wasn't sure what that meant for her. Would she be able to commit? Would she be able to stay?

Finally, after what felt like forever, she asked softly, "If I say yes... what difference will it make?"

My heart leapt.

With all the excitement in the world, I replied, "I'll study harder than ever! I'll fix everything in life! I'll throw the biggest party my friends have ever seen!"

I was breathless with anticipation.

And then, slowly, shyly, with a little smile in her voice, she said the words that changed everything:

"Yes, Subhransu... from my side, it's a yes."

I didn't even wait for another second. I hung up, ran to my room, and shouted to my friends, "SHE SAID YES!" And then... I danced like a madman.

That night, I hosted a party, one full of ***BOBAL*** *(our code word for unfiltered joy and celebration). It was, without question, one of the happiest days of my life.*

But the happiness came with a twist.

When I told my friends about the call, they weren't satisfied.

"Wait," one of them asked, "She said 'yes,' but did she say, 'I love you'?"

"No," I replied, "She just said yes."

"Then what's the big deal?" another one smirked. "Anyone can say yes. It doesn't mean she loves you. You've failed, my friend. The mission isn't complete."

And just like that... I was back in dilemma mode.

They were right. She hadn't said the three magic words. "I love you." That mattered to me. I needed to hear it. Not because I doubted her feelings, but because I wanted it to be real, complete, undeniable.

So, the next day, I began my next mission.

I told her, "If you truly love me, you have to say it. Say the words. A simple 'yes' isn't enough."

She giggled and replied, "Why don't you understand? If I said yes, it means the same thing!"

But I wasn't falling for that.

"Nope. I can't just assume. If it's love, you have to say it."

She hesitated, smiled, and said, "Okay fine, tell me how to say it then."

So, I broke it down.

"Say 'I'..."

"I."

"Now 'Love'..."

...Silence.

"Say it!"

She laughed nervously. "He..he... I can't. I feel shy."

Was it so hard for a girl to say those three words? I wondered.

It took me **22 days**. *Twenty-two days of playful teasing, pleading, and patient waiting.*

And finally..., finally..., she said it.

"I love you."

I stood frozen, grinning like a fool, heart pounding like a drum solo. I wanted to give her the tightest hug, a kiss on the forehead, and freeze that moment in time forever.

But reality came crashing back.

"Kya aapka phone khatam hua? Dusra customer wait kar raha hai!" the booth owner shouted. (Translation: Is your call over? There are other customers waiting!)

I blinked. I was still in the booth, still holding the receiver, people staring at me from outside. I looked at the clock, I had been in that booth for ***three and a half hours.***

And just like that, I chuckled to myself, still dazed, still smiling. That moment? That was the real beginning of my love story.

— *"Speak your truth, it takes courage to confess, and even more courage to accept the answer with respect. Words like "I love you" are precious, but they mean most when backed by steady, everyday actions. Gentle patience and playful persistence open hearts more than force or demand ever will. Protect the friendship first, it is the soil where love grows; celebrate the beginning and help it bloom."*

8

The Moment of Truth

Classes for the second semester had begun, and I was living in a constant state of bliss. I was in seventh heaven. Subhadra and I had become close again, like before, but with something new blossoming underneath the surface.

Every morning, I would travel nearly ***9 kilometers*** *to her bus stop just so we could go to college together. She waited for me daily, and we would take the bus together with the wind, the road, and the silent joy of unspoken feelings between us. Sometimes Sangita joined us, making the journey more vibrant, but even in her presence, Subhadra and I shared a quiet world of our own.*

Ironically, we talked more over the phone than face-to-face. Both of us were shy, painfully so. We'd walk to class and return without saying much, but those silences were golden. They carried more weight than words ever could.

Then came one unexpected moment.

It was a lazy morning when the ***STD booth boy called out to me*** *from the ground floor.*

"Subhransu! Phone call for you!"

I rushed down, hoping it was her and yes, it was.

"Are you coming to college today?" she asked sweetly.

I decided to mess with her a little. "Nope, not coming."

"What? Why? Is everything okay?" she asked, surprised and worried.

"Yeah, just... something came up," I said, planting the seed of my little prank.

"Wait, are you in Bhadrak?"

"Yes," I replied, casually.

"No way! You were here yesterday. How did you reach Bhadrak overnight?"

"Fine, if you don't believe me, here, talk to my nephew. He's standing next to me."

I quickly changed my voice and, imitating a little boy, said in the cutest tone, "Kya bol rahe hain aap? (What are you saying?) Namaskar aunty (Aunt)."

She was completely convinced. She even asked my fake nephew if he had eaten. Then she said, "Okay, beta, give the phone back to your uncle."

Still playing along, I returned to my voice and asked her, "What did he say?"

"Nothing much," she giggled.

"Well, he's crying."

"Why?"

"Because... no one is giving him a pappy (kiss)," I replied, grinning.

She laughed, slightly stunned, then replied, "Well, you give him what he wants!"

"I don't know how," I teased. "I've never had one. Maybe you can show me how to give one."

Without hesitation, she replied, "Don't worry, I'll teach you."

And just like that, my heart went into overdrive. Goosebumps. Electric jolts. Butterflies doing backflips. I couldn't believe what I was hearing. Was this really happening?

Before I could ask more, she said, "Papa's (Father) here, I must go. Bye!"

"Wait, wait! Thank you!" I said quickly.

"For what?" she asked.

"Nothing... I'll tell you tomorrow in college."

"Fine! Bye! Take care!"

She hung up. And I just stood there in the booth, staring at the wall, imagining what tomorrow could bring.

The next day, I couldn't go with her in the morning due to some personal work. I reached college straight and went to class. She was already seated in the **second row**, *with her friend beside her. I quietly slipped into the third row, right behind her.*

It was the Mechanics of Materials class, a subject already boring enough, but that day, I couldn't have cared less. I was too busy admiring her.

Her head slightly tilted forward, her neck exposed just below her ear; glowing, soft, framed by strands of silky hair. The beauty of that moment was indescribable. That small patch of her skin shone more radiantly than any lesson in mechanics ever could.

I leaned forward slightly, gently blew a puff of air at her hair, and then... I couldn't resist. I picked up my pen and lightly touched her neck.

She jerked around and exclaimed, "Ahhhh!"

The class went silent.

The teacher looked up. "Subhadra, what happened?"

She stood up, turned back once, glanced at me, and said, "Nothing sir... maybe something touched me."

"Okay, sit down," he said.

After she sat, she glanced at me and smiled.

That smile gave me the courage I needed.

I tore a small piece of paper, wrote "I love you", and passed it to her discreetly.

She took it with grace. A few moments later, she passed it back.

When I opened it, my heart skipped a beat, it wasn't just a note. It was a ***beautiful sketch of two hearts intertwined*** *with our names written inside.*

I was floating. That feeling was beyond words.

I extended my leg under the bench, trying to reach hers. She noticed. She adjusted her posture, extended her foot slightly back, and... our legs touched.

I quickly removed my shoes and socks with my feet to feel her warmth. Her skin was soft, warm, comforting. I was completely lost in the moment.

Then **class ended***. Students got up. She got up too, without looking back. Everything had returned to normal. But not for me. I sat there for a moment longer, stunned by how beautiful life could be.*

Later that day, we shared an auto-rickshaw on the way home, as usual. Two other passengers were squeezed in beside us. Her stop came before mine.

I leaned closer and whispered, "Do you remember why my nephew was crying yesterday?"

She smiled, "No, you tell me."

"He was crying for a kiss," I said mischievously, looking away with a fake innocence. "Not me though..."

"Oh really? So, you weren't crying, huh?" she teased. "Why didn't you just say you were?"

I turned back to face her, and it happened.

She gently held my hand, pulled it toward her lips, and kissed both sides of my palm.

Soft. Warm. Real.

I froze. My heart was racing. I couldn't speak. Couldn't blink. It was the most romantic moment of my life.

Before I could say a word, the auto stopped at her junction. She smiled, stepped out, and called back, ***"Bye Subhransu… see you tomorrow!"***

I sat there in stunned silence, watching her walk away, wondering if that moment had happened. My hand still tingled with the memory of her lips.

That night, I barely slept. I wrote her a letter just to say thank you. Thank you for making me feel seen. For the magic of that moment. For being the first girl to ever kiss me.

And yes… I slept that night with a smile on my face ***at 4 AM****.*

— "Treasure the small, honest moments, they become the memories you carry for a lifetime. Gentle gestures often mean more than grand promises; let tenderness, not theatrics, lead. Always respect each other's comfort even as you celebrate closeness, consent and care matter. Be grateful and present: love grows in quiet attention, not in haste or show."

9

Leap of Love

As days passed, our bond deepened. I started going to her home frequently. Our college usually ended by 1 or 2 PM, and we'd return together, halting at her stop. Sometimes, instead of going straight home, we'd take small detours quiet nearby places just to continue our conversations, just to stretch the time we had. After two to three hours of roaming or talking, she'd go home, and I'd return to my hostel.

Often, I'd have lunch at her place. We'd chat, laugh, and share stolen moments before I quietly left around 3 or 4 PM before people in her colony began wandering out for their afternoon routines.

With each passing day, my attachment to her grew... and so did my possessiveness.

I began claiming invisible rights over her, placing silent expectations in every part of her life. I thought of her constantly, obsessively, my world was centered around her. Just the idea of living without her sent chills through my bones. I couldn't imagine waking up in a world where she wasn't mine.

The thought of life without her wasn't just painful, it felt impossible.

Her smile, her voice, her presence, without them, I would be nothing but a breathing shell. My obsession took over. I watched her every move. Not to control, but because I genuinely wanted to protect her. To keep her safe, untouched, unbothered. I wanted her to belong only to me; mind, heart, body, soul.

I became jealous of everything. Her friends. Her classmates. Even the sunlight that touched her skin. Her laughter, if shared with someone else, felt like a betrayal. If she so much as spoke sweetly to another boy, a storm would brew inside me.

I wasn't in love anymore; I was drowning in a whirlpool of possessiveness and insecurity.

I wanted her attention, her focus, her everything. And if I ever felt like she gave a little less, just a little, I'd get upset. Angry. Arrogant. I began pulling her away from her friends, from anyone I thought was taking my space in her life. I forgot about her individuality, her freedom, her dignity.

{And today, with all the sincerity in my heart, I want to say sorry. Publicly. Honestly. It was one of the biggest mistakes I made during that phase. I loved her more than my life, yes. But I was so blinded by that love, I failed to see what I was doing to her. I tried to mould her, to change her, to cage her spirit and for that, I will always be sorry. She didn't deserve that. Yet, she stayed. She bore my anger, my irrational behavior, and my overwhelming need for control with grace, with patience, and with quiet love. For that, I respect her deeply.}

I tried to transform her into my vision of beauty; smart, confident, healthy, and entirely devoted to me. But she was changing, in the opposite direction. She grew thinner, quieter, paler. Her fear of society and our secret love kept her constantly anxious.

She feared being caught, feared her father's anger, feared what would happen if anyone found out. And it broke her. While I was full of dreams and romance, imagining her as my future wife, she was shrinking under the weight of social pressure.

In my heart, I believed love should come first. That she should put me before everything. I was convinced that if we were to marry as I always envisioned then like every traditional Hindu wife, she should consider her husband (me) as everything.

But we were drifting.

Her fears pulled her one way, while my expectations pushed her the other. I expected her to do things my way, say things my way, live her life for me. And when she didn't, I got frustrated. Angry. Disappointed.

We argued often.

She never argued back, she would only cry. And each tear should've shaken me awake. But I was caught in a mindset I didn't know how to escape. The worst part? She thought I didn't love her anymore. She thought my anger meant indifference. But I loved her so deeply, I just didn't know how to show it right.

And I never told her. I expected her to feel my love even in my silence, even in my scolding.

*I dreamed of showing her off to the world, introducing her proudly to my mother as my beautiful, smart, "***Sarba Guna Sampanna Bohu***" (an ideal daughter-in-law with all the virtues). I imagined people admiring us, envying our love, thinking we were made for each other.*

But things weren't going as I imagined.

She still wore the same clothes I didn't like. Still travelled by overcrowded buses to save money, despite my repeated requests to take an auto. I couldn't stand the thought of strangers brushing against her in packed buses. So, eventually, I started traveling with her just to keep her safe. She didn't think much of it. To her, it was casual.

But to me, every inch of that bus, every unintentional touch, felt like an invasion. She was 20. But sometimes, she acted like a carefree child. I, on the other hand, could feel the gravity of everything.

And then came the day I can never forget.

The worst day of my life.

We were returning from college, and every bus was full, so full that you couldn't even step in. After missing several buses, we finally boarded one, already stuffed to the brim.

In that bus, women stood near the front, and men toward the back. She was pushed toward the front cabin, and I, by the force of the conductor and crowd was shoved to the rear.

From the back, I watched helplessly as she stood there, squashed between people. No space to move, to breathe. Panic flooded me. Rage, helplessness, fear, it all rushed in at once.

Desperately, I started pushing through the crowd, elbowing my way forward, shouting, "Let me pass! I need to go there!"

I reached her, finally. She stood wedged between the seat's handle and a sea of strangers. I stood behind her, shielding her, trembling, not with anger, but with sorrow. I began to cry.

Right there. In that overcrowded, suffocating bus.

But she didn't notice. She stood still, oblivious, unaware of the storm inside me. I wiped my tears quickly and started a light conversation, hiding everything behind a smile. But inside, I was shattered.

When we got off the bus, I kept my emotions buried. I only said, "Please avoid traveling like this. Let's just take an auto next time, it's more comfortable."

She simply nodded.

That day... I realized something painful: even though I loved her fiercely, maybe I had failed to love her rightly.

— *"Love that cages will wither; protect without possessing, freedom is the truest gift you can give someone. Notice when your love makes the other person smaller; love's task is to nourish, not to reshape them into your ideal. When fear or anger rules you, choose apology and humility, they rebuild trust far quicker than pride ever could. Be present with kindness, listen more than you command, and let change come from care, not control."*

10

The Cost of a Promise

As days passed, my possessiveness only grew stronger. I wanted to see her near me always. I couldn't bear the thought of her getting too close to anyone else, especially when she expressed her natural sweetness and charm. That was just who she was, soft-spoken, kind, effortlessly lovable. But in my head, it felt like a violation. I kept expecting her to understand how it made me feel... yet she never changed her ways.

And I never truly expressed it either. I held those emotions tightly inside me, locked away, buried, but they burned. They would come alive at night in my dreams, haunting me with fears of something going wrong, something terrible happening to her. I was terrified of losing her, of her drifting away. Some would call it insecurity. Maybe it was. But at that time, it felt real... uncontainable... like a part of me I couldn't control.

Yes, I believed she was mine. ***Only mine.***

I didn't mind people being around her, but I hated when she was overly friendly or close. I wanted her to draw a line, to keep a distance, not for herself, but for me. But despite my countless silent pleas, she never understood the reason for my frustration. Or maybe she did but chose not to act on it.

Still, time kept moving. Seasons changed their colors. We flowed with them, unsure of where we were headed.

Her health, meanwhile, was slowly deteriorating. She was getting thinner by the day, eating less, stressing more. And yet, she continued to fast on religious days. **Ekadashi** *was one of those sacred days for her, she wouldn't eat anything except a few fruits, and that too barely enough for a child.*

I kept asking her to stop. I was worried. I begged her to consider her health. But she never listened. She was firm in her beliefs, and once she decided something, that was it, no one could change her mind.

So, I did what I thought might help.

I began fasting too.

Not because I believed in the ritual, but because she did. I wanted to show her what it was doing to her. I thought maybe if I suffered with her, she'd understand my concern.

The truth? I couldn't even handle four hours without food. But for her, I pushed through 24 hours.

It was painful, mentally and physically.

But even after knowing how much it affected me, she still didn't stop fasting.

That broke me.

It made me feel invisible. Useless. As if my care, my sacrifices, me, meant nothing to her. I started to wonder, Was I the wrong person for her? Was I loving someone who didn't understand what love meant to me? I was emotionally drained.

Then came the second-semester exams.

Three days before our first paper, she planned to fast again, this time for two full days because of back-to-back festivals. I asked her not to. I pleaded, reminding her how close exams were, how she needed her strength.

But she remained firm.

So, in my frustration, I said, "Fine. Let something serious happen to me. I leave it to God."

I fasted again. And this time, I didn't just skip food, I also stopped studying. My anger consumed me. I wanted her to feel my pain, to realize what she was doing, not just to herself, but to me.

On the third day, I collapsed.

I had to be hospitalized, hooked up to an IV, exhausted, dehydrated, and starved, not just of food, but of emotional understanding.

Still, the next day, with the saline barely absorbed into my veins, I forced myself to attend the exam. I hadn't revised a thing. I scribbled what little I remembered from before and left the hall in an hour and a half. This repeated for every subject.

She kept looking at me from across the exam hall, confused, maybe concerned but by then, my anger had snowballed into something darker. And when the results came, the reality hit harder than anything else.

I had scored just 60%. Worse, I got a back paper in Basic Electronics.

It was the first time in my life I had ever failed anything.

I was devastated. Broken.

But I stayed silent. For her, I bore it. I told myself, It's fine. I love her. That's enough.

But the truth? She didn't understand. Or maybe I never explained it the right way.

Looking back now, I realize, **she wasn't wrong either.** *She was just being who she was, devoted, spiritual, committed* *to her own principles. But at that time, I couldn't see that. I only saw her refusal to bend for me, and it crushed me.*

We lost some of the most beautiful days of our young love to arguments, misunderstandings, and the ego of wanting to be understood first.

If only we had listened to each other... really listened... things might have been so different. So much better. We could have created memories filled with laughter and love instead of fights and frustration.

But still, life teaches you in strange ways.

That painful phase taught me something invaluable:

"Let life unfold as it comes. Don't force the moments. Just cherish them, gently."

— *"Don't let possessiveness be the price of love, true care protects freedom and dignity. Sacrifices offered to prove a point become wounds; choose empathy and healing over stubborn tests. Listen before you judge; honest communication and humility can save what pride quietly destroys."*

11

Miles Apart, Hearts Close

One fine morning, we decided to do something wild... something we'd never done before.

We planned a secret trip to ***Puri, Jagannath Dham****, without informing anyone in her family. We told them we were headed to college, but instead, we set out on an adventure of our own.*

We caught an early morning bus, hearts full of excitement and just a tiny bit of nervousness. The bus was jam-packed, people squeezed in shoulder to shoulder, voices overlapping, the heat rising. There wasn't a single seat available, so we stood for a while, stealing glances and trying to hide our excitement behind shy smiles.

After some time, the conductor kindly arranged one seat for us. Without hesitation, I offered it to her. But true to her nature, she refused. "You sit," she said, pushing me gently. I insisted, and she insisted harder. Eventually, we settled the battle by sharing that one seat, half each.

And just like that, with a little discomfort and a lot of love, ***our journey began****.*

It felt magical.

That was the ***first time*** *we had gone somewhere together, just the two of us, outside the world's watchful eyes. It felt rebellious... but innocent. Risky... but right. And we were both quietly thrilled about it.*

When we reached Puri, we walked hand in hand down the ***Bada Danda (The Grand Road)****, heading toward the sacred* ***Jagannath Mandir (Lord Jagannath Temple)****. The air was filled with chants, the smell of incense, and the energy of countless devotees. We offered our prayers, tied a sacred thread on the* ***Kalpabata Tree (The Ritual Wish Tree)****, believed to grant wishes and silently made our own.*

Then we headed to the ***sea beach****.*

Ah, the sea... its breeze, its roar, and the sun dancing on the waves. It felt like time had slowed down just for us. We didn't need words. We just were. Sitting there on the sand, laughing, talking, stealing glances, it was the kind of peace you don't find often.

By late afternoon, we started our journey back.

On the return trip, the air had grown cooler. She started to shiver lightly, rubbing her arms for warmth. I took off my jacket and offered it to her. But, of course, she refused.

Instead, she looked at me, smiled mischievously, and asked, "Shall we both wear the same jacket?"

Ha... ha... ha…

That moment, so sweet, so silly, so purely us.

After some back-and-forth, playful nudges, and shared giggles, we finally squeezed into my jacket, shoulder to shoulder. I don't even know how we fit. But we did. Snug, close, hearts racing, breaths mingling.

You can imagine the scene, two awkward college kids squeezed into one jacket, giggling like fools, while the whole bus stared at us.

But did we care?

Not even a bit.

We were lost in each other, cocooned in our little bubble of warmth. There was no bus, no crowd, no staring faces. Only us and the ***fragrance of love*** *that surrounded us like a soft, invisible cloud.*

That day?

It became ***the most wonderful day of our lives up until that point****, not just because of where we went, but because of how we felt.*

Unapologetically in love. Free. Unfiltered. Ourselves.

— *"Sometimes the simplest moments, shared with honesty, become the most sacred memories of life. Love doesn't need luxury or perfection, it just needs presence, trust, and the courage to be real. When hearts are pure, even a single shared jacket can feel warmer than the world itself."*

12

The Language of Silence

Time passed, and our relationship began to harmonize beautifully. The chemistry between us had become so natural, so organic, it felt like the very air around us carried the fragrance of our love. People around us could sense it, it was in our eyes, our smiles, the way we were always somehow drawn toward each other.

We had become so emotionally dependent that even a day apart felt unbearable. Silence between us, even for a few hours, was torturous. We had reached that fragile yet powerful point in love, where the heart beats for just one person and everything else becomes secondary.

And then... life threw us a test.

Our summer training period was about to begin.

She was assigned to ***National Thermal Power Corporation (NTPC)****. I was sent to* ***Talcher Thermal Power Station (TTPS)****, nearly 50 kilometers apart. We wouldn't be able to see each other or talk for an entire month due to our tight schedules and, worse, the lack of mobile phones back then.*

It felt like the sky had fallen.

Neither of us could process it. It was our first true separation. She left for NTPC with Sangita, and I was scheduled to leave for TTPS three days later. But those three days? Oh, they were hell for both of us.

When I finally reached TTPS and somehow survived the first night, I knew I couldn't stay put. The next morning, I signed my training attendance sheet, took permission from the manager and left. I boarded a bus, burning under a 45-degree summer sun, and by 2 PM, I reached NTPC.

But I had a problem, I didn't know where she was staying.

I only vaguely remembered her mentioning that she'd be staying at her uncle's house inside the NTPC township. So, I did what any hopelessly-in-love guy would do, I walked.

House to house. Lane to lane. Just praying that somehow, she might come out. That I'd catch a glimpse of her.

Nothing.

By evening, I was exhausted, sunburned, and emotionally drained. I slumped onto the bench of a small tiffin shop and ordered something to eat, more out of survival than appetite.

The shopkeeper turned out to be from my native area. That small coincidence felt like fate tossing me a lifeline. I opened to him. Told him I was looking to shift my training to NTPC and didn't know where to stay.

He told me there was no hotel around, and his shop barely had enough room for one person, he slept inside at night. But he offered me the bench outside his shop to spend the night.

I accepted without a second thought.

That night, under the open sky, I lay there, surrounded by mosquitoes, choked by exhaustion, but holding onto a single hope: that somehow, I'd find her.

At 2:30 AM, it began raining.

I stood in the downpour for hours, unable to go anywhere. No shelter. No sleep. Just a heart that refused to give up.

The rain stopped around dawn. The shopkeeper woke up, and by 7 AM, he took me to meet an NTPC officer. I shared my situation, begged him to help transfer my training. He asked me to come back during office hours. I waited, hopeful.

But that day, the officer was too busy. I had no choice but to spend another night on that same roadside bench.

The next day, something changed.

As I wandered through the township again, I saw ***Sangita*** *walk into a house. My heart raced. Could it be?*

I couldn't risk entering. Her uncle was strict, and if he suspected anything, it could destroy everything. But now I knew where she was. That was enough for now.

I waited again through the night.

And the next morning, as I walked toward her uncle's house... I saw her.

She was walking out, with Sangita by her side.

My heart skipped. And when she saw me, she ***ran*** *toward me, without a second thought. No fear, no hesitation. Just raw, desperate love.*

She threw her arms around me, and I held her tightly, our eyes full of tears we couldn't hide anymore.

But the universe, as always, was watching.

"Sangita!" a voice yelled. "Subhadra, your uncle's son is coming!"

And just like that, our moment shattered.

We separated instantly. I turned around and began walking, pretending not to know them. Her tears flowed like a storm, faster than I could process, faster than I could wipe away.

I waited at the nearby chowk. Minutes later, they came. And we got to speak, briefly. I told her about my efforts to transfer my training, and her face lit up. Her relief was visible. We promised to meet again.

But the transfer didn't happen immediately. So, I returned to TTPS... but not in spirit. I was already at NTPC.

For the next **seven days**, *I did the impossible.*

Every morning, I signed attendance at TTPS, then took a bus under the merciless 46-degree heat and travelled 50 kilometers just to spend a few minutes with her at lunch in the NTPC canteen. Then I'd return to TTPS in the evening.

Sometimes I missed her. Sometimes I'd arrive and she'd already left with her group. But I kept going.

On the 7th day, I finally received my training acceptance letter from NTPC.

I was overjoyed.

But another twist: they placed me in a different group since I joined late. That meant she and I wouldn't be together in training. I begged the officer, saying I didn't mind losing those 7 days, just let me be in her group.

And he agreed.

From the next day, we trained together.

We were beyond happy.

Eventually, her group completed the training, and she was ready to return home. My training still had a week to go, but I couldn't let her travel back alone. So, I went with her, leaving my training incomplete.

As a result, I didn't receive a completion certificate from **either** *TTPS or NTPC.*

But I didn't care.

What mattered was that we had been together.

And through it all, our love only grew stronger. We were no longer just a couple, we were two souls tangled in something deeper, something we couldn't define... only feel.

Oh God... even now, as I recall it, that chapter of my life flickers in my memory like an old film reel, raw, wild, and heartbreakingly beautiful.

But wait... I can't stop here. I must tell you what happened next. Because what came after, was something I'll never forget for the rest of my life.

Forgive me for going on, but I must share it with you...

— "True love isn't measured by distance or time, it's proven in the courage to show up, again and again, no matter the odds. When the world tests your bond, let faith and effort speak louder than fear or comfort. Love built on sacrifice and patience outlives every separation, it becomes a language only hearts can understand."

13

Midnight in the Rain

It was one of those rare days when college ended early, around 2 PM. We decided to make the most of it, to escape the chaos, to just be with each other. We took an auto and headed to ***Khandagiri Caves****, a scenic spot popular among visitors and lovebirds alike.*

After reaching the hilltop, we found a cozy place with a panoramic view of Bhubaneswar. The city sparkled beneath us, like a carpet of diamonds under the golden afternoon sun. We sat there, soaking in the view, talking, laughing, stealing glances, and feeling our hearts inch closer. Slowly, the casual conversation turned into something softer, more intimate. Like the other couples around us, we found our moment, holding hands, sharing quiet affection, letting the stillness speak.

Eventually, drawn deeper into the romance of the moment, we wandered to a more secluded spot within the cave's embrace, seeking silence, just us, just love.

She sat under a small tree. I lay in her lap, her fingers gently stroking my hair. We whispered, laughed softly, shared secrets and smiles. I had never felt so safe, so seen, so loved.

Until I noticed something.

Two eyes. Blinking. Watching us from the shrub nearby.

At first, I thought I was imagining it. But no, there it was again.

I whispered to Subhadra, "Someone's there..."

She stiffened. Before we could move, three men emerged from different directions, surrounding us.

My heart stopped.

I was terrified, not for myself, but for her. I didn't know what their intentions were, and all I could think was, please, God, let her be safe.

They grabbed my hand and started interrogating. Who we were. What we were doing. They threatened to inform our parents, saying they knew who we were. I pleaded, begged them not to. I told them we were students, that this could ruin everything, our reputation, our future.

But they wouldn't budge.

They demanded ***Rs. 5,000/-*** *in exchange for their silence.*

My mind raced. We didn't have that kind of money. I didn't know what to do, until an idea struck me.

I told them we would get the money the next day from our parents. But to assure them, I handed over my ***college identity card****, explaining that without it, I wouldn't be allowed into class. I promised to return with the money and asked them to hold onto the card until then.*

Miraculously, they agreed.

The moment they walked away, we ran. Like an express train, hearts pounding, faces flushed, breathless. We didn't look back.

We never returned their money. And we never forgot that day.

It had been the ***most terrifying, unforgettable*** *day of our lives.*

That night, I found myself walking alone, lost in thought, heavy with emotion. A storm brewed in my mind and echoed in the sky. Somewhere between guilt, fear, and heartbreak, I wandered into the middle of the highway.

A loud, furious horn blared. A massive truck was inches away from hitting me.

I jolted out of my thoughts, suddenly, violently pulled back into reality.

I realized I had gone to Subhadra's home earlier that night, hoping to see her, but she hadn't opened the door. And now, my heart was racing again, not from fear, but from pain. I turned and walked home, slowly, silently, arriving at 2:30 AM. I parked my bicycle, shut the door gently, and crawled into bed.

But sleep refused to come.

I lay there, broken.

I stared at the ceiling, the clock ticking away, 3:00 AM… 3:15… 3:30…

Suddenly, I made up my mind.

I had to see her.

I didn't take my bicycle this time. My younger brother had to attend class in the morning, and I didn't know when, or if, I'd return.

So, I walked.

Alone. Along the National Highway. Seven to eight kilometers in the rain. No umbrella. No plan. Just hope. Just love.

By 4:30 AM, I reached her neighborhood. The rain had softened into a mist. The sky had begun to lighten, the early whispers of dawn. The world was silent, still asleep. I rang her doorbell with a racing heart and trembling fingers.

An old lady answered groggily. "Who is it?" she asked in a half-sleepy voice.

Panic. *Who is she? Her neighbor? Relative? What if she finds out? What if she tells her father?*

But then I realized: maybe this was why Subhadra didn't answer my knock the night before. Maybe the presence of this woman had stopped her. Maybe I had misunderstood her silence.

My heart sank. I had spent the whole night cursing her in my mind, doubting her, painting pictures of betrayal. I felt so ashamed.

"I… I'm Subhransu," I stammered. "Can I meet Subhadra?"

The woman blinked, still groggy. "Yes, she's inside. Come in and sit."

I stepped in, unsure, haunted by the previous night's emotions.

A few moments later, **Subhadra came out** of her room, sleepy eyes, tangled hair, wrapped in her night shawl.

She saw me and froze.

"Subhransu… *you?*"

There was shock, nervousness, a little fear, but mostly worry. She looked into my eyes and must've seen the chaos within.

Before I could say a word, my tears broke free.

Without hesitation, she rushed to me, took my face in her hands, and pulled me into her lap, **caressing me, kissing my forehead, wiping every tear**. Like a mother consoling her wounded child. Like a lover repairing a broken soul.

At that moment, I melted.

All my pain, fear, and anger vanished in the warmth of her touch. I felt like I was home.

I held her tightly and told her everything, what I had gone through the night before, how I walked through the storm, the pain of thinking I had lost her.

She listened, then held me even tighter.

"I'm sorry," she whispered. "But maybe it was good that I didn't open the door last night. What if that aunty had seen you? She might have told Papa (Father)."

We both nodded.

We understood.

Sometimes, the universe protects us in the strangest of ways.

— "Sometimes love is tested not by distance, but by danger, and the way two hearts protect each other in silence. Never mistake someone's quietness for indifference; often, it's their way of keeping you safe. When storms come, don't curse the delay, some detours are divine protection in disguise."

14

Career or Love?

"Give me one cake…" I casually told the canteen boy, standing in the veranda with Santosh and Satyajit. The college campus was buzzing; it was **recruitment season**. One of the top MNC software companies had arrived for a placement drive, and everyone had started registering for it.

We three were about to register too, right after grabbing a quick bite from the canteen.

I took a bite of the cake.

Suddenly, something hit me.

Not physically… but mentally.

A strange wave of uneasiness rippled through my body. I felt cold, unsteady, like something was wrong. Really wrong.

I murmured to myself, “What is this? Why am I feeling so unstable suddenly? Is something happening to Subhadra…?”

And just as I finished that thought,

A voice shouted from near the main staircase: **“Subhransu!! Where are you?! Come quickly! Subhadra is losing consciousness!!”**

That moment?

It was as if a nuclear bomb had exploded inside me. My hands froze. My mind went blank. My heart stopped.

The thought I had a second ago… was **real**.

I dropped everything and ran. No looking back. No thinking.

When I reached the stairs, I saw two of my friends carrying Subhadra down. She looked completely disoriented, crying, shivering, barely able to keep herself together.

I rushed to her.

"Leave her… I'm here now. Everything will be fine," I told them, trying to stay strong even though I was breaking inside.

I held her in my arms, gently settled her onto a sofa in the waiting lounge near the principal's office. I gave her some water, started massaging her forehead, stroking her back, whispering softly to calm her down. Slowly, she began to settle. Her breathing eased. Her tears slowed.

Just then, **Gupta Sir**, our Placement Officer, arrived.

He asked, "How is she now?"

I nodded, "She's feeling better, Sir. Still weak. She needs rest."

He looked at his watch. "Subhransu, the recruitment process has just started. Let her rest here. You should come and attend the interview."

I looked at him.

And then I looked at her.

She was still lying there, fragile, scared, unwell. She needed me. How could I leave?

I asked, "What about Subhadra? Will she be allowed to sit later once she feels better?"

Gupta Sir paused. "If she can't attend now, she won't be able to sit later. The process won't go on beyond today. That's just how these companies work."

Then he added, gently, "But you must go. This is a golden opportunity. Don't miss it."

And in that moment, I decided.

One that surprised even me.

I said, calmly and firmly,

"Sir, if she can't sit, I won't either. If we sit, we sit together. If not, then not at all. Please excuse me. I can't leave her like this."

He stared at me, speechless.

It wasn't rebellion. It wasn't drama.

It was **love**, unshakable, honest, and raw.

He didn't say much after that. Just looked at us for a moment, then said, "Alright. Take care of her. Call me if there's an emergency."

And then he left.

Later, I found out that day changed something in his mind. He understood the depth of our relationship. He'd seen something real in a world full of distractions. Something that stayed with him.

A few months later, during another campus drive, he helped me in a way I'll never forget.

I had appeared for the interview, performed well, but was unexpectedly rejected. Confused, Sir went straight to the recruiters and asked what had happened.

Their answer?

"He's underweighted. We require at least 51 kg. He mentioned 49 kg in his application." They were just noting what we had mentioned, not weighing.

Sir came to me and whispered, "Just go tell them it was a typo. Say you're 53 kg."

I followed his advice, went back in, and told them the correction.

And I got selected.

That day in the waiting room, sitting beside Subhadra while others rushed for placements, I missed a company, but gained something far greater.

Her trust.

Sir's belief.

And a memory of love that was far more meaningful than any job offer could ever be.

— *"Success built on compassion lasts longer than success built on competition. Choosing humanity over opportunity may cost you a job, but it earns you respect that no salary can buy. When life makes you choose between love and ambition, choose with heart, not haste, for true success includes both."*

15

Between Two Worlds

After my campus selection, I moved to Mumbai. Life was transitioning, but not without its share of turbulence. While I was trying to settle into my new job and surroundings, I received news that shook me, Subhadra's parents had started searching for a groom for her.

The moment I heard it; a wave of anxiety swept through me. What should I do? What should we do? We were completely lost and puzzled. We had always planned to talk to her parents at the right time, once things were a little more stable in our lives. We hoped that once they knew, they would stop looking for a match for her. But that "right time" was nowhere in sight.

The truth was, I wasn't ready. My family was going through a crisis. My father's heart condition was worsening. Two of my elder sisters were still unmarried, and their marriages were a top priority. I couldn't even imagine adding the weight of my love story to my family's shoulders at that moment. I feared that revealing our relationship then could bring disappointment and chaos into a home already burdened with enough.

So, I thought, let me wait. Just until my sister gets married. Then I'll tell them everything. She, too, tried delaying things on her end. She gently urged her parents not to rush into finding her a groom, hoping to buy us time.

But fate had other plans. Just a few days later, everything came crashing down. One of her close friends, knowingly or unknowingly, spilled the secret to her parents.

It was like a natural disaster, sudden, sweeping, and destructive. Her father and uncle were furious. Her father immediately demanded that she call me. But I was in Mumbai, barely a few weeks into my first job, still in probation, with no possibility of taking leave.

I asked her to explain the situation to him, that I couldn't come just yet, but would visit as soon as possible. She did, but her family was too hurt, too angry, too overwhelmed to accept it calmly. For them, the storm had already hit, and my absence only made things worse.

What followed was perhaps the hardest time of her life. Her home became a battlefield. Her mother blamed her constantly. Her father's health began to deteriorate under the emotional weight of it all. And as always, it was society's opinion that loomed large in their minds, how could they let their daughter marry someone from a different caste, a different background?

Her mother kept telling her that if anything happened to her father, she alone would be responsible. The emotional blackmail, the pressure, the guilt, it was unbearable. Subhadra was broken. Day by day, it crushed her spirit. She cried often, kept to herself, and lived in fear of what might happen next.

Every day, they pressured her to call me. To get things "settled." Her father, despite his pain, didn't want to see his daughter suffer for life. So, he told her to call me, talk to me, fix things fast. But his inner turmoil was visible. He didn't want to disappoint his relatives or society either. The whole situation was a tangled mess of love, tradition, fear, and expectation.

Meanwhile, I was thousands of kilometers away, helpless. I couldn't be there for her physically. I couldn't fight her battles. All I could do was call her whenever possible, talk to her softly, try to give her strength. But in my heart, I knew, no words from a distance could ease her pain.

Her uncle began calling me often too, asking me to come and talk face-to-face. But each time, I apologized, helplessly. I was still trying to find my footing in a new city, a new job, and a life that seemed to be tearing in two directions.

I knew how much she was suffering, and yet I couldn't do anything but listen, helplessly, hopelessly, as she cried on the other end of the phone.

That was perhaps one of the darkest, most helpless stretches in both of our lives. And even today, the pain she endured during that time lingers in my heart like a scar I couldn't heal.

After Two Months

Two months after the chaos, I got selected for the O.P. Jindal Group of Industries, a reputed multinational company. The posting was near my hometown, in Jaipur, Odisha, and I shifted from Mumbai with a sigh of relief. But that relief didn't last long.

Soon after joining, I got absorbed in the whirlwind of project work. Days blurred into nights, and I had barely any time to think about the discussion pending with Subhadra's family. But the weight of it sat heavily on my chest. My mind was caught in a constant loop, what to do, what not to do. I was utterly confused.

My elder sister was still unmarried, and her wedding was the immediate priority for our family. So many proposals had come and gone without any conclusion, and this uncertainty scared me even more. How could I talk to my parents about my own love life when the responsibility of my sister's marriage still rested on my shoulders?

I couldn't sleep properly at night. My heart was burdened with both guilt and fear.

Then one day, Subhadra called me. Her voice was nervous. "Papa (Father) wants to speak to you. He's asked me to call you home."

My pulse spiked. I was instantly unstable. Around the same time, her uncle also called and asked me to visit their home for a discussion. I had no choice. I nodded and said, "Yes, I'll come next week."

And with that commitment, I stepped into a week filled with sleepless nights and restless thoughts. How would I face them? What would I say? What would they ask? What if they forced me to inform my parents? That would be a disaster, both for my family and for us. I wasn't ready. Not yet.

The thought of being asked to get married immediately, or worse, without my family's consent, haunted me. I couldn't imagine doing something that went against my values. I deeply respected my family, my traditions, and my love for Subhadra. Getting married in secret wasn't an option. That wasn't love, that was cowardice, and I didn't want our story to begin with guilt.

I mentally prepared myself for every possible question they might throw at me. Finally, the day arrived. It felt like walking into a lion's den.

I parked my bike outside and pressed the doorbell with a pounding heart. Their living room was modest, sofa, dining table, and a small bed placed in one corner. Her uncle sat quietly. Her mother and aunt were inside the kitchen.

"Please sit," her uncle said politely. I took the seat, doing my best to hide the fear bubbling inside me. My face wore a mask of forced calmness, but my heart was racing faster than ever.

A few minutes later, her aunt walked out with a plate of fruits. I offered my pranam; she gave a small nod and returned to the kitchen. But the question lingering in my head was, **where was Subhadra?** And even more pressing, **where was her father, the one I feared most in that moment?**

Then, breaking the silence, her uncle asked the question I had been dreading:

"Do your parents know about your relationship with Subhadra?"

I took a deep breath and replied with the courage I had summoned all week. **"No, not yet."**

Shock flashed across his face. Her mother looked visibly disappointed. She frowned and said, "You haven't told your family yet? Then how do you expect anything to move forward? We're planning her wedding this month. We can't wait forever."

I tried explaining calmly, "My elder sister is still unmarried. As the elder & responsible son, it's my duty to settle her marriage first. It's not the right time for me to bring this up at home. Please understand."

Just then, her father entered and sat down. Without pleasantries, his voice thundered, "If you had the courage to fall in love with her, why don't you have the courage to tell your parents? And if not, then do something to assure us that this relationship will materialize. We can't just sit here and wait endlessly."

His words felt like a dagger. I was confused, were they agreeing or disagreeing? They wanted to fix the marriage quickly but were also furious at the same time.

I repeated what I had come to say: "I love Subhadra. I am committed to her. But I cannot disclose this to my family until my sister is married. Please trust me."

Her uncle insisted again, "If you can't talk to your family now, then do a court marriage. Keep it secret for now and disclose it later when the time is right."

I shook my head firmly. "No. I will not do that. I want to marry her with everyone's blessings, in the proper way. Whether it's a love marriage or arranged, I want it to happen respectfully. Why should love to be treated like a mistake or a crime?"

I could see they were still unsure. They didn't trust me yet. But I stood my ground with humility and conviction.

I continued, "Please give me time. Once my sister is married, I will talk to my family and take things forward with full responsibility. I will never betray your trust."

They didn't seem convinced, but they didn't push further either. The conversation ended, tense but complete. They performed the basic formalities with me as they would with any prospective son-in-law, but I could see it in her father's eyes, he didn't like me. Not one bit.

Still, I had no choice but to accept the moment as it was. I stood up, offered my namaskar to everyone, and quietly left.

Back at the hostel, I told no one what had happened. I kept playing the conversation again in my head, wondering,

"What now?"

— *"Love demands courage, but true courage lies in choosing patience over rebellion. The right path may take longer, but a union blessed by honesty and respect stands firmer than one built on haste. When caught between duty and desire, choose integrity, because love without dignity cannot last."*

16

The Weight of Family

A few days later, her uncle called me again.

"Subhransu, have you decided anything? When is your sister's marriage going to happen? We can't wait anymore. My brother is deeply troubled. He's not able to sleep until her marriage is finalized."

He poured out his worries. I listened in silence, then replied with the same conviction I'd held all along, "Please wait just a little longer. I promise, the day my sister gets married, the very next day I will speak to my family and inform you. But before that, I just can't."

My words left her family disheartened and frustrated. From their side, it seemed like a hopeless scenario, Subhadra had outrightly refused to marry anyone else. She made it clear that if she ever got married, it would only be to me.

That only intensified the pressure on her. Her mother, especially, lashed out at her in every conversation, on every occasion. Subhadra was drowning in her own home, living through a storm of disappointment, blame, and helplessness. She cried endlessly, yet there was nothing I could do to ease her pain. And slowly, she began pushing me harder to speak to my family.

But what she couldn't see, what she perhaps couldn't fully understand, was that I was trapped too. It's often said, *only a woman carrying a child knows the pain of childbirth*. That's exactly how it was. We were both in pain, both under pressure, but unable to truly comprehend each other's burden.

My situation was slightly more complex. My elder sister was still unmarried, and I was younger than her. How could I walk into my house and say, "I want to get married"? I knew, absolutely knew, my parents wouldn't take it well. Even if I raised the subject, there was no way they'd agree to go ahead with a proposal so suddenly, especially to a girl from a different caste.

So, I stayed quiet, biding my time, trying to hold everything together with patience. I was also searching desperately for a groom for my sister, reaching out to friends, relatives, online matrimonial sites, every possible source. But nothing was working.

Meanwhile, Subhadra kept pushing me to tell my parents. I knew her fears. Perhaps she was beginning to lose trust in me. Perhaps she worried that I might run away, abandon our love. And truthfully, I didn't blame her.

In moments of frustration, I said things I never meant. Harsh words. Things like, *"If your family is in such a hurry, go ahead and marry someone else. I can't tell my family right now."*

That broke her even more. But I said it not from the heart, but from helplessness. And I hated myself for it.

One day, I felt like I was going mad. I was so lost in my thoughts, so mentally shaken, that I walked out of the bathroom mid-shower, wearing only my towel and undergarments, roaming around the hostel like a sleepwalker. My friends stared at me in disbelief.

On one side, she was desperate and hurting. On the other, I was helpless and stuck. My father's heart condition. My sister's delayed marriage. My family's financial condition and expectations from me. My promise to Subhadra. My inability to sleep. It was chaos.

I couldn't even eat on time. Breakfast was skipped altogether, or I'd eat something around 3-4 PM. Dinner would be around 11-12. My life had shifted entirely into "PM mode." No food. No peace. No stability. Just guilt, pressure, and emotional wreckage.

And still, every morning, as the sun rose, so did the pressure from her end. Calls, tears, pleas, fights. I'd promised her back when we first fell in love that our marriage might take five years, maybe ten, but it would happen. I had responsibilities to take care of first. She had said she would wait.

But that promise faded once her parents began pressuring her.

Every day she reminded me of her pain. And every day, I tried to explain mine. I was growing more restless, irritated, and broken. Sometimes, I told her cruel things just to escape the moment.

But deep down, I knew, I loved her with all my heart. I wanted her in my life. I wanted her to be my wife, my queen, my guiding light. I never imagined she would become this impatient… or maybe I never realized how much she was suffering.

Finally, in May 2009, my sister's wedding was fixed and solemnized. The moment that happened, I knew it was time. I had promised Subhadra's uncle that once my sister's wedding was over, I would tell my family about us.

But that wasn't easy.

How could I, in a deeply traditional family rooted in conservative values, announce that I had been in a love relationship for years, without their knowledge? That too in a family where my mother trusted me blindly.

She had always believed that I would never hide anything from her. I had made that promise to her since childhood: *"Ma, I'll never take any step in life without your blessing."* She believed me. She had faith in me. She thought her son would never betray her trust.

And now I had to shatter that illusion.

A few days before this, my elder sister had done a little "spying" and told my mother about my relationship. My mother had asked me directly, and I had flatly denied it. I lied to her face and said, *"No Bou (Mother), I promise you. I have no such relationship. Don't believe Didi (Sister). Trust me, I'll marry the girl you choose for me."*

And she believed me. She even scolded my sister and said, *"I know my son. He'll never do anything behind my back."*

That lie still haunts me.

But at the time, I wasn't lying entirely. I had made another promise to myself: *When the time comes, I'll ask my mother to meet Subhadra. If she agrees, I'll marry her. If she doesn't, I'll convince her in the most respectful and polite way. I won't marry until she agrees. One day will come, she will be convinced.* That was my plan. That's how I justified it.

Now the time had come. My sister was married. My promise to Subhadra's uncle was due.

And I couldn't avoid it any longer.

With trembling hands and a heavy heart, I walked towards my mother to tell her the truth that would either break us apart or bring us closer than ever.

— *"The heaviest burdens in life are not carried on our backs, but in our hearts, between love, duty, and truth. Lies told to protect peace often wound deeper than the truth ever could; speak with courage, but with respect. Real strength is not in hiding pain, but in facing it with honesty and faith in those who love you."*

17

A Mother's Tears

"Bou…(Mother…)" I called softly from the doorway.

(We call our mother as *Bou* in our local tradition.)

She was busy in the kitchen, stirring something on the stove, when she looked back and replied, "Hmm? What is it, beta (Son)?"

"I need to ask you something," I said, almost in a whisper.

"What happened? Ask me, what's bothering you?" she asked, without pausing from her cooking.

"No, Bou. Not like this. You must promise me… you won't get angry," I said firmly, my voice still low, but trembling.

She turned around, surprised. "Why would I get angry? Okay, I promise. Now tell me."

I looked down. "No Bou, you must promise again. A strong promise."

She softened, a bit emotional now. "Okay, strong promise. Now speak, please."

Taking a deep breath, I finally said the words I had been carrying for so long, "The girl Didi mentioned the other day... it's true. It's real."

For a moment, there was complete silence. Then,

Clang!

The steel utensil in her hand fell to the floor, echoing like a bomb. And before I could even react, she collapsed right where she stood.

"Bou!" I shouted, rushing to hold her. I caught her mid-fall, my hands trembling as I helped her onto the bed.

Her eyes were wide, flooded with tears. She wasn't unconscious, but she was overwhelmed, shocked beyond words. Silent sobs wracked her body. Her chest heaved, her face pale.

I sat beside her, speechless and helpless. I had no idea what to say or how to calm her down. Watching her cry like that, as if something precious had been snatched from her, tore me apart. I felt like the worst son alive.

This was the same woman who had given me everything, her time, her strength, her unconditional love. She never let me cry, never let me suffer even for a moment. And today, I had become the reason for her tears.

I hated myself for it.

But what was I supposed to do? I loved *both*—Subhadra and my mother, with every ounce of my being. I wasn't choosing between right and wrong. I was stuck in the middle of the ocean, standing on two boats drifting apart, knowing that if I chose either, I would drown.

That entire day passed in silence.

That night, around dinner time, Bou came to my room and said, "Come, have your dinner."

Her voice was tired. I followed her to the dining room, hopeful that maybe things had settled.

She served the food quietly, without looking at me. I watched her walk away to her room, still wiping tears from her face. She hadn't said a word to me, not a single word about what I'd said earlier.

It crushed me. That silence felt heavier than any scolding could ever be.

I sat there, staring at my plate. My appetite had long vanished. I rested my head on the table and cried silently. After a while, I washed my hands and threw the untouched food into the bin.

Later, I found out she hadn't eaten either.

My father, as usual, ate his dinner. Bou hadn't told him anything. I thought maybe the storm would pass by morning. Time heals, right?

That night, I hardly slept.

Around 7 AM, I gathered some courage to go to my parents' room. I thought maybe I could strike a different conversation, something casual, something to read the mood.

But what I saw inside broke me.

Both my parents were sitting on the bed… crying. Like children. Holding each other, weeping in silence.

I froze.

And I ran.

I ran back to my room and buried my face in my pillow, crying like I hadn't in years.

They didn't say anything. They didn't even yell. That silence, that heartbreak, spoke louder than words. I wanted to scream, *"I haven't done anything wrong! I haven't broken your trust! I haven't promised anyone anything. I just want you to understand."*

But I couldn't. I had no voice left.

Days passed like that. My father didn't speak to me at all, not for a whole month. He avoided me, pretended I didn't exist. That was the most painful part. I had never felt so invisible.

But gradually, Bou began speaking to me again. Softly, distantly.

One afternoon, I sat down beside her and spoke from my heart.

"Bou… it didn't happen intentionally. It just happened, slowly, without either of us realizing it. We started as friends, and then... we became close. I didn't do anything to bring shame to you or our family. I never made a commitment to them. I told them I'd speak to you first, and *only if you agreed*, would I proceed. That's still what I want. You go meet her once. If you don't like her, I'll tell them it won't happen."

She didn't respond. She just sat there, processing everything in silence.

Those days were the slowest-moving days of my life. Each hour stretched endlessly, full of unspoken words and unanswered questions. But I waited… because what else could I do?

Then, as the pressure from Subhadra's family began to mount, I finally told Bou over the phone, "Please go once. Just meet them. If you agree, we'll proceed. If not, I'll let them know it won't be possible."

She paused, but didn't say no. Deep inside, I knew, my mother would never ruin someone's life or disrespect my relationship with Subhadra. She may have been hurt, but she understood my love.

Eventually, she convinced my father.

Though they both carried their pain silently, they began the process. Traditionally, the girl's family makes the first move in a marriage proposal. But in this case, Subhadra's family refused to initiate it.

They said, "Your son made the choice. Let him complete it."

So, with a heavy heart and the last remnants of his pride, my father, who hadn't spoken to me for weeks, picked up the phone and made that call. That call which cost him so much.

And I knew… even though they had agreed, they were doing it out of love for me, not because they were convinced. They were still hurting.

But I didn't have a choice anymore. Subhadra had reached her breaking point. And the process had to begin, one way or another.

I carried the guilt of that pain with me every single day.

— "A parent's tears are the purest reminder that love, and pain often speak the same language. Honesty may break hearts for a while, but hiding truth breaks them forever. Seek understanding, not victory, because real love unites generations, it never divides them."

18

The Interview

After a long, emotionally exhausting wait, the day finally arrived, a day that felt nothing less than a judgment day. The day of selection, of suitability, of fate.

My father, along with a small "troop" of close family members, my mother, sister, uncle, went to her house to *see* the bride. It was supposed to be a simple, formal visit. No decisions were to be made; it was just an initial meeting to assess compatibility. But for me, it was a crucial moment, the first move in turning our love story into a socially accepted one.

I've always believed in the saying, *"Baat karne se baat banti hai" (things begin to fall into place once conversations start)*. And this visit was just that: the beginning of a much-needed conversation. I didn't want any drama, no sudden declarations, no runaway love stories. I wanted it to happen smoothly, respectfully, and within the structure of tradition, without damaging anyone's dignity or values.

That's why, despite the pressure I constantly faced from her family, I stuck to my principles. I refrained from doing anything rash, knowing well that a single wrong move could scar the future for both of us.

So, the day arrived. My family visited her home, and as I waited anxiously, I prayed for one thing: let it be positive. Because if it wasn't, I truly didn't know what I would do next.

They were received warmly. Her parents treated my family as if it were a typical arranged marriage meeting, formal yet friendly. It felt surreal to me, that after everything we'd been through, we were finally on this path. My mother and sister met her separately. As expected, my mother, ever particular about appearance, wasn't quite satisfied. She didn't say much, but I could read her expressions like a book. "She's too thin," she murmured later, her tone layered with subtle disapproval.

Still, they didn't openly reject her. Everyone politely said she was "nice," "fine," "well-mannered", but I knew what they really meant. It was the same concern I had been voicing to Subhadra for years. Her physique had become fragile over time, and I had always urged her to take better care of her health. But she rarely listened.

After they returned, no one brought up the meeting much. But in a private conversation with my elder sister and brother-in-law, I got the real sense, it was a 50-50 kind of situation. Not a “yes,” not a “no.” But something had begun. And that gave me hope.

Next, it was *their* turn.

They were to visit our home to see the "groom", *me*. I was nervous. We lived in a rented house, having moved out of our ancestral home when I was just five months. In fact, we didn’t own a house at that time. That bothered me a little. But then I thought, *why hide the truth? Let them see me and my life as it is. If they accept me, it should be for who I truly am, not for a facade.*

On the chosen day, under a bright sun, they arrived, an entire *platoon* of about twenty people! It felt like a mini wedding procession. I was amused, overwhelmed, and mildly terrified. *Was this a meeting, or a grand celebration already?*

But one thing was clear: I had to impress everyone, within just one hour.

I kept telling myself, *Subhransu, this is the most important interview of your life.* Not one interviewer, but a whole *panel*. From her father to her uncles, from aunties to elderly neighbors, everyone had come. And I had to charm each one according to their role and personality.

Her uncle might need tea without sugar for his diabetes. Her aunt would probably want to see how respectfully I behaved. Her father, God, he would be the toughest one. And of course, I had to win over her mother too.

I was multitasking mentally, calculating who wanted what, who needed extra attention, and who might be the one secretly judging me the most. It was overwhelming. But there was no escape. I had to face this *interview panel* with confidence and grace.

When I was finally called in, I walked into the room with folded hands, offering a big *namaskar* to everyone together, and then individual greetings to each of the "designated officers," as I had classified them in my mind. Ha ha!

Suddenly, the room went silent. A subtle, tense fragrance of anticipation filled the air.

The questions began.

Name? Age? Qualification? Job? Salary? Family background?

I answered them all calmly, honestly, respectfully. I wasn't trying to impress them; I just wanted them to see me as I was.

But throughout the whole interaction, her father remained silent. Not a word. Not a question. Not even a smile. His expression remained unreadable.

That made me nervous. Eventually, the meeting came to an end. No dramatic scene. No sudden outbursts. But also, no declarations.

Later, I learned, the result was *positive*. Yes. Positive!

Despite everything, both families had agreed to move forward. A suitable date was discussed for our engagement and marriage. And in that moment, a sparkle of joy ignited within me. I could feel it, our love, once doubted, questioned, and hidden, was now stepping into the light.

The wait was finally over. My queen and I were finally walking toward the life we had always dreamed of, together, openly, with blessings.

And now, we simply waited for that one beautiful day to arrive...

— *"When love chooses patience over rebellion, even fate begins to listen with kindness. Truth, respect, and humility can open doors that force never will, win hearts, not arguments. The most beautiful unions are those that honor both love and tradition, proving that dignity and devotion can walk hand in hand."*

19

Destiny's Date

It was the 28th of May, 2010, the date both families had finally agreed upon for our wedding.

And to my absolute surprise, and perhaps a little divine orchestration, it was the *same* date we had fallen in love for the very first time… seven years earlier.

Yes, 28th May 2003 was the day my heart quietly chose her. And 28th May 2010 was the day we officially became one. What are the odds? It wasn't just a coincidence. It was something far more powerful, a sign, a blessing, a message from the universe.

To me, it was proof that when love is pure and true, even time bends in your favor. That when you truly want someone, not out of possession but out of devotion, God listens. He may test you, stretch your patience, shake your strength, and throw you into chaos... but eventually, He gives you what's meant to be yours.

So, my friend, this story is not just about me. It's about love in its truest form.

Love that waits.

Love that survives.

Love that heals and never hurts.

If you truly love someone, with all your heart, soul, and sincerity, *life* finds a way to bring you together. That's not just a belief; it's the truth I lived.

So, love deeply. Love yourself. Love others. Love your well-wishers. Love this world.

Because love… is everything.

You don't have to fight the world to win it. You just must love it enough to make it yours.

Be a human first. And let love do the rest.

— ***Subhransu Sekhar Ojha***